A light bulb was placed by someone.

That someone placed it there for a reason,

to bring in light.

People can place darkness too,

in order to spread darkness.

But few hang up lightbulbs of change.

Because change disperses light and darkness.

What you bring to the world is your choice.

Unless you're controlled and can't place anything.

Then, in that situation, nothing is placed.

The Uncontrolled

Zachary Astrowsky

YA
Astrowsky

zachary.astrowsky@yahoo.com

https://theuncontrolled.wixsite.com/website

Follow on Instagram @the_uncontrolled_novel

A portion of the proceeds of this book will be donated to Reading is Fundamental (RIF), the nation's largest children's literacy non-profit organization. www.rif.org

Book design by Jason Simon. Instagram @simplesimongd

Photograph by Jen Wilbur. Instagram @bluestitchaz

August 2017

This book is dedicated to my mom for supporting and guiding me through my life.

CHAPTER 1

"School is so tedious. I don't think I can finish all of this annoying homework by myself," I said to my best friend, Chase. Chase took the hint. "Well, why don't you come over to my house? I think my mom will be okay with me tutoring an idiot." That comment clearly deserved an elbow-jab to Chase's side. Drawing his arms across his tight athletic shirt, he doubled over, his moppy blonde hair hiding the pain on his face. We immediately burst into laughter, like we always did, completely oblivious to the golden rays of sunshine dancing across the schoolyard this afternoon. When I straightened my 5'8" frame from this hunched laughing state, Chase was stretching his arm over his afflicted side and staring past me. He liked puzzles so I knew one was about to come up.

"Have you noticed how our teachers hardly ever talk?" he began, "They just point to things on the whiteboard."

I had noticed. "Dude," I replied, "Isn't it obvious? Maybe they don't have much to say because we already know everything."

We exploded into laughter again, and then as if on cue raced ahead toward the school buses. The school buildings and offices became a blur and the high fence that surrounds the school came into sharp focus. I fixed my eyes on that fence and picked up the pace but I could tell Chase was still recovering from our extremely witty repartee. By the time we got to the parking lot we were sweating and other kids were crowding around the buses. We fell back into a walk and turned onto the old cracked sidewalk that ran along the fence. Suddenly I could feel unusually cold afternoon air pass under my clothes and I shivered. Chase must have felt it too. "3, 2, 1, go!" he announced as he broke into a sprint. *Challenge accepted,* I thought to myself.

Ignoring someone shouting, "no running," we ran as fast as we could to the bus labeled with the number 410. I easily maneuvered myself around hundreds of kids walking in different directions while Chase struggled to keep up, politely stopping for every kid that got in his way. Not surprisingly, I made it to the yellow bus first. Chase liked to wear athletic shirts but he wasn't especially athletic. And I liked to rub his face in the irony of his friend in the preppy collared dress-shirt trouncing him in every impromptu race.

Chase breathed heavily and bent his fatigued body over, putting his hands on his knees. Sweat was pouring off of his forehead and pooling on the ground. I had to admire his shameless attempts to beat me. "You ok, buddy?" I asked, with just a hint of gloating.

"I'm fine," he snapped back, "if only my backpack wasn't so heavy."

I was just about to land a crushing "yeah, right," when the driver chimed in: "Hey, kids, come on. We don't have all day!" We climbed up the steep metal stairs that welcomed us to rows of rambunctious middle-schoolers. The bus driver threw us one of those weird smiles as we passed by him and found our usual seats in the back of the long bus. The air conditioner was blasting and I felt a chill again.

As the bus rattled to a slow crawl out of the parking lot, we kicked our backpacks under the seats in front of us. "I'm going to miss the first two periods of school tomorrow because I have to get my fourteen-year-old vaccine shot from that ancient doctor with the crazy white hair in that creepy office that smells like donuts," I told Chase, hoping he wouldn't detect my life-long dread of needles.

Chase's eyes got big, "No way! I'm getting my shot there tomorrow, too!" With that, we talked on and on about horrendous giant needles filled with vanilla custard and enormous vats of grease in a back room. We plotted to take over the place and get to the bottom of that donut smell. I started to feel a lot better about my fate, as if I had some control.

After five bumpy blocks, the bus stopped at a sign that read "Apple Tree Blvd." We picked up our backpacks and ran to the front of the bus to exit. We descended the stairs and landed on a cracked concrete sidewalk just like the one at school. "I have a project to do in Science, but it's not due until Monday," I said as Chase tightened down the straps on his grey, worn out backpack.

"Yeah, I heard kids talking about that. I'm glad I don't have the same teacher as you," Chase replied cheerfully, "I can help you if you want. What's it about?"

I hadn't read the whole assignment yet so I gave him the short version. "It's about some erosion process," I said, taking in the block of identical triangular homes neatly lining the street to the right and left of us as far as the eye could see. I was grateful for the offer but I couldn't help giving my friend a little ribbing: "Do you *know* anything about erosion?"

Before Chase could answer, I dug out my small cell phone and dialed my mom's number. After a few rings the phone's computer voice told me to leave a voicemail. "Just in case you were wondering, I'm at Chase's and will walk home. See you soon. Love you. Bye." I stored the phone away in my backpack and we kept walking.

"I remember learning about erosion in class. Pretty easy subject," Chase said, with his hands stretching outwards as if smoothing over a surface. Chase was extremely smart, but his long hair and athletic shirts didn't fit the mold. I was probably the only one at school that recognized Chase's intelligence. I liked to be a

5

leader so people always turned to me for help. But after two years of friendship I had to admit that Chase was just smarter about some things.

The street seemed to go on forever and each house we passed seemed a little shabbier than the last. Chase and I lived on similar streets and lived fairly close to one another in a city called Grand Sile. The major roads and stores and exciting places were on the north side, but the south side was where most people lived. On the outskirts of Grand Sile were quiet towns like Hiltire, Den Valley, Amber City, and Kingstown. For years on the weekends my parents would take me on slow drives through these other towns. They would look around and whisper to each other. When I was ten, we were practically crawling through Amber City, each of them scanning the houses and my mom writing notes. I asked them if we were moving but they just sped up and changed the subject. It never came up again.

Amber City was the least populated of the suburbs and it was the closest to the doctor's office where we were going tomorrow for our vaccine shots. I didn't really want to live in the suburbs even though the buildings and houses out there were being renovated and brought up to date. Around here, on the other hand, the homes were plain and simple, or as my mom would say, homogeneous. "Here's a beauty," Chase stated ironically as we arrived in front of his home.

His two-story house was made of wood and brick and looked exactly like one of those cartoon houses you would see a kindergartener draw. It was just like all the other houses on the block except for the potted sunflower next to the door. The sunflower was taller than me and packed with seeds. Chase must have put it there I thought because his dad was always away and his mom was pretty "buttoned down," as my mom would say. Catching me staring at this botanical stand-out, Chase seemed to read my mind, saying, "She's already moved it twice because she thinks potted flowers are against the homeowner's association rules."

Chase's mom greeted us with a weird, fake smile as we trudged through the elevated door. Her smile wasn't unusual to us. Most people we encountered smiled similarly. It was the typical Grand Sile fake smile, so we thought. We smiled back and walked through the sunny kitchen and then straight up a flight of stairs to Chase's room. Chase went up the carpeted stairs by skipping one step and landing on the next. I walked up the steps one by one, like a normal human being, noticing the extra wear on every other step. Chase must have been going up this way for a long time. His room was a decent size, like mine, and the walls were decorated with sports junk. His floor, nightstand, and dresser were covered with books. We flung ourselves from the doorway onto the bed, competing to see who had the longest leap. Being taller, I won this one too, which I rubbed in as we fished out our notebooks and started on homework.

After about an hour of toiling on homework, we were finished with it. The football shaped clock on Chase's nightstand said it was 4:00 p.m. so we agreed to play video games on Chase's "new" ZV40, which was actually released three years ago. Chase never had the latest and greatest so he used irony and jokes to pretend he didn't care. I thought his put-on cluelessness was brilliant and funny but I tended to stay a little closer to reality. Truth is I didn't need to pretend--my parents had a decent amount of money and treated me like gold. Neither one of us had any siblings so in spite of our differences we were close, more like brothers than friends. And I always felt like we were different in mutually beneficial ways.

We went downstairs into Chase's basement to play on his gaming station. The basement was full of antiques and old pictures stacked in piles in one corner of the room. We sat down on decrepit chairs in front of a relic of a TV and were immediately hypnotized by the screen. After about an hour of csgo that seemed more like five minutes, I was snapped back into sleepy south Grand Sile by the smell of hotdogs descending from the kitchen. "Crap! I have to get home," I blurted out as I grabbed my backpack and practically ran out of the house.

My walk home from Chase's was terrifying. It always was but it was starting to get dark which made me dread it even more. Fortunately, I knew, based on prior trips, that it took only about seven minutes, most of which was through an alley that joined our streets. Unfortunately, the alley is why it's a terrifying walk. This alley seemed especially dangerous. Mysterious shadows moved across the walls and grew darker and longer with every step. I gulped and stared straight into the uninviting narrow path in front of me. Grey walls that seemed to bleed black tar towered above

9

on both sides and I could not see the other end. I felt myself tensing up and I trembled as I stepped into the alley. I could hear my own breath and the squeaking of my sneakers on the hard damp concrete. It had to be ten degrees colder in there. For the first time I noticed a little camera on the alley wall and wondered who was watching and why. When I finally made it to the light at the other side, I exhaled heavily realizing I had been holding my breath for quite some time. I was sweating and shivering at the same time. It was like my body was remembering something about this alley that my mind had somehow shut out.

I pulled myself together and decided I was stupid for being scared of a familiar little alley. I took a left turn away from the alley and walked toward my house. I couldn't wait to be home. My backpack felt like it weighed a hundred pounds and that got me thinking about inventing an anti-gravity backpack. It would lighten the weight of backpacks by diverting gravity with quantum magnets. I couldn't believe no one had thought of this already and I was sure this invention would make me rich and famous. I basked for a moment in the thought of becoming an inventor and helping the world with some really cool innovations, but that didn't last long. My house, which was now right in front of me, seemed deserted and unfamiliar. There were no lights on at all, which was very weird. My parents should have been home and by now making dinner and watching the evening news. Maybe they went out to dinner, I tried to reassure myself. But something just seemed wrong, I could feel it.

I moved toward the door as quietly as I could and without a sound, tried the knob. It was locked. I retreated to the sidewalk near the streetlight and searched my backpack for my house key. I found it, zipped up my backpack, walked back to the door and inserted the key into the small slot in the doorknob. Suddenly, my arm pulled back violently, as if it had a mind of its own. Yes, it would be better to use the back door instead, I thought, as I shoved the key into my pocket, threw my backpack over the low rusty fence by the front door, and then leapt over the fence after it.

Our backyard is a little too small for our massive pool, which is blue-green and murky this time of year. It was so dark back there that I had to tiptoe along the back fence through the landscaping to avoid falling into the pool. After crossing the

11

grassy hill on the north side of the pool, I reached the back door. Slowly, I unlocked the door that entered into our newly remodeled kitchen. We had new quartz countertops and a new kitchen island with subway backsplash tiles and new high-end appliances. My brain was scrambling for answers. *Why would my parents go out to dinner when they finally had the kitchen of their dreams?* I cracked the door and peeked in. I immediately spotted two figures--my parents--each tied to a chair.

I also noticed another set of figures standing close to my parents, facing the front door. Luckily their backs were to me. *Good call right arm,* I thought. If I had gone in the front door, I'd be screwed. These guys seemed to be waiting for me to come home so I quickly and silently crouched behind the new island, trying to get a sense of what was going on. I leaned out slightly and saw that one of the men was holding something, what looked like a hypodermic needle. *Are they going to poison my parents? Damnit,* I screamed inside my head.

I was trying not to panic but I knew I had to do something fast. I leaned back against the island and looked around the kitchen for a solution. The answer was right there in front of my face. One of the low cabinet doors was slightly ajar. This was the "special" cabinet that was always locked and I was warned of being permanently grounded if I ever even thought about trying to open it. I slid closer and opened the cabinet. It contained three metal boxes and two of them were open and empty. The third was still closed and had some weight. I pried off the lid, which was hard to do in total silence, and inside was a small grey matte pistol. It was loaded. *No wonder I'd be grounded!* I figured the intruders had the two missing weapons so I tucked the gun into my belt and pulled a big knife from the block on the counter. I thought I had a brilliant idea: I'll distract the men, cut my parents loose with the knife, give my dad the gun in case anything goes wrong, and we'll run to a neighbor's house and call the police. I took the key from my pocket and threw it to the left of the men.

It seemed to work. The men were startled and headed into the hallway to look for whatever was the source of the noise. When they were out of sight, I rushed toward this incomprehensible scene: my parents gagged and tied to chairs. Their eyes were wide with terror but the knife cut the ropes quickly and I was moving fast. We'd be out of here in no time.

13

CHAPTER 2

The room was spinning and my knee was killing me. A dark blurry image hovered overhead. As I struggled to focus, I could see it was my mom shaking me. *How long had I been out? A week? Days?* I was on the floor and the room around me was slowly getting brighter. I was home, on the floor next to a broken chair, my mom was holding my hand and she looked like she had been through hell. *Where's dad?* I could think this but the words weren't audible. I looked around and could make out two lumps nearby oozing blood. *Please tell me dad isn't one of those lumps*, I thought, realizing that no one could hear me. My mom, sensing that I was coming to, and confused, squeezed my hand tightly and spoke softly and slowly. "John, you're okay. You passed out. Your dad is okay. I'm okay."

What happened? I started to recall the scene I walked into. I tried to save my parents but I blew it. These guys were going to kill us, but they didn't. *Why were they here? How did we escape? Who shot them?* I kept trying to speak but my tongue wasn't cooperating. I tried to get up, but my legs weren't cooperating either. I must have tweaked my knee when I passed out. Fighting tears of frustration, I just lay there and tried to put the pieces together. It was still dark outside and my mom was wearing the same clothes so I couldn't have been out long. If there was a gun battle, we won. The two men that threatened us were dead. Just then my dad appeared with a glass of water and they both helped me to my feet. "Thanks, dad," I heard myself say out loud, and they both beamed as we shuffled over to the chair that my mom was very recently tied to.

After a few minutes of dabbing my forehead and neck with a wet paper towel, my mom took my hand again and fixated her eyes on my dad's, and then mine. She was wearing her "very serious look," which is what Chase called it when she got mad at us one time for taking a bus to Amber City to see a movie without telling her. "We need to talk," she said, "Let's go outside and get some air."

"Yeah," I replied, so happy to hear my own voice, "I have a few questions."

This time I was able to get up on my own and my mom and I walked out to the table by the pool while my dad stayed behind. I assumed he was going to do some cleaning. *What do you do with dead bodies?* I wondered, being careful not to say it out loud. The thought of disposing of dead people started to make me sick and I felt myself on the verge of passing out again. I was never good with seeing blood or wounds, but this was really over the top. Goosebumps popped up all over my skin as a chill spread throughout my body. I quickly stumbled to the grassy hill and threw up. *I can do this* repeated in my mind as I returned to the pool and dropped my feet into the cold water.

My mom sat down beside me and started to explain the inexplicable, "There's a lot you should know before tomorrow. Your father and I are among a few people in the world who know about this so listen carefully to what I am about to tell you."

I swallowed hard and tried to listen, but my mind was racing. "Did you know those men?" I blurted out, suddenly pissed that they might have known this was coming.

17

She went on in a hushed voice, "When a child turns fourteen, like you are about to, they get the last of their shots. Vaccinations, you know? No big deal. For you, John, that day is tomorrow. What most people do not know is that instead of receiving an immunization this time, the fourteen-year-old gets a Tracker for Globe or "T.F.G." It's like a biological chip that makes it possible to track you, even control you, later in your life."

I shook with confusion as my mom rubbed my back and brushed my hair with her fingers. My mind was such a jumble of questions that I had no words. *This is crazy! What is she talking about? I come home from school, I'm scared half to death, and now I have to listen to this crazy explanation!* It was hard to pay attention, much less understand it all, so I just sat there quietly swishing my feet in the water and watching the waves ripple out.

"I know that it's hard to process all this information right now," she continued, "but we don't have a choice anymore. Ten years ago, your dad accidentally found the T.F.G.'s database while we were researching unordinary things in our world. It was just a list of names, and where these people were and what they did for work. But it seemed odd because we knew some of the people on

18

the list and had seen them change in very extreme ways, around the same time. So we decided to hack into their system to see what information they were hiding. At first, we weren't sure what we were reading. There were maps, mentions of doctors, descriptions of chemical compounds, and details of a campaign to vaccinate everyone in the greater Grand Sile area by the end of that year. There was more information, but their firewall seemed to heal itself and we were never able to get back in. And we've tried for years."

Numbness overtook me. I was in a semiconscious state and I could barely see the fence on the other side of the pool. I wondered what time it was and realized I hadn't eaten anything in maybe seven hours, which had to be a record for me. I wanted a pop tart more than anything in the world. Then I heard footsteps coming from behind and I jumped, splashing water from the pool onto my mom. I turned around expecting to be killed, but it was only my dad, holding pop tarts. "Sorry," he said, "I thought you might be hungry."

"John," my dad said as he sunk into one of the chairs by the pool, "The men that showed up here tonight were trying to

19

give your mom and I that shot. Somehow, they now know that we are 'out of control,' as it happens."

My mom let out a half-laugh and started to wash her face with pool water. "I think we must have set off alarms when we cancelled your 'automatic vaccination appointment' four times," she mused out loud.

"Well, however they know, they know," my dad chimed in, "and when they realize that their henchmen are dead, we're all in very serious danger. We need to disappear to save ourselves, but that also means we have failed to save humanity and the future from this grotesque abuse of power!"

I could tell he was torn about what to do. My mom could see I was struggling to understand how sticking around would even be an option. She stood up and went to my dad's side as she prepared to lay it out for me. "Our plan for the last ten years," she said, "was to get back into their system and find out what their chemical compound is and how it works. We thought if we knew how it worked we might be able to counteract it somehow--maybe find an immunization for the immunization."

"And now, thanks to your quick-thinking tonight, John, we *have* the shots that they intended to give us," my dad interjected. "If we could get this stuff to a lab, we could test it and at least find out what it is. I know one such lab exists in the basement of the immunization clinic where you are supposed to get your shot in…" He looked at his watch in disbelief, "Holy cow, less than eight hours."

The pop tart must have done the trick because I was starting to think clearly again. It must have been about midnight. I couldn't think about what happened in all that missing time. "Should I show up to get my shot and somehow get you into the building without anyone seeing you?" I asked.

My dad looked thrilled that I was the one to bring up that possibility. "I was just thinking the same thing," he said quickly as he looked to my mom for permission.

"Chase has an appointment tomorrow too," I said excitedly as a plot was forming in my head. "Maybe I can catch a ride with him and his mom, and then ask for directions to a bathroom after I sign in…tell them I'm a little queasy about shots or something like that." *Which is true*, I was thinking. "I'm sure I can slip out of sight and find the back door. There's always a back door, right? What if it's locked? I was thinking I could let you in the backdoor but it might be locked on both sides."

"Yeah, there are security cameras back there too," my dad said, hope draining from his face.

"Wait," my mom broke in, "we've cased this building and first of all, it's old. The basement still has those old casement windows that pop open from the inside. There are two on each side if I remember correctly, well away from the cameras. John, if you can get to one of those windows and pop it open, we can get in. The greater problem is how we let you go to that appointment and still prevent you from getting that shot. I mean, so far there is no antidote. It's a huge risk."

We were all quiet for a minute, trying not to let our fear devour our plan. I had the added problem of pushing down the urge to laugh out loud when my earlier conversation with Chase popped into my head. *I guess we're going to get to the bottom of that donut smell after all, my friend.* I composed myself just as my dad started talking crazy, but this time the good kind. "John, we have some firecrackers. After you open the window," he said, emphasizing *after,* "can you light one or two in the bathroom on the main floor and create some commotion? I imagine there will be an alarm and everyone will have to exit the building. Whatever you do, you cannot go into that room and get that shot."

"I can't let Chase get the shot either," I said, "I've got to tell him, right? Will he believe me?"

My parents looked at each other and were silent for another minute while they tried to work out this wrinkle. "We don't want *anyone* in that clinic to get a shot tomorrow," my mom said breaking the silence, "I think you need to be the first one in, and all of this has to happen very quickly. Chase's mom is being tracked, so we can't get her involved. But yeah, if you can trust him, Chase should know at least enough to stall if we can't get the fire alarm to go off in time. We will get you to that appointment early and stay out of sight until you can get a basement window opened. You better try to get a little sleep, John, while your dad and I try to get everything together. We don't have much time and frankly, we can't be sure that the T.F.G. doesn't already know the fate of those men that attacked us last night and planning their

23

CHAPTER 3

I tried to get mentally ready for the rough day ahead, hoping Chase would understand all of this. Sleep seemed like an impossible prospect. I was anxious and scared and sad. I thought about how much my parents had gone through trying to keep me safe from this, and about all the people deprived of real futures, and how they don't even know what was happening. I thought about Chase's mom and all the other parents with those weird smiles, probably because they were controlled by the T.F.G. *Were they all as detached from their own kids as Chase's mom and dad?*

Exhaustion engulfed me and I drifted off into some kind of half-sleep, in spite of the insanity of the last six hours, or maybe because of it. In the midst of this sleep, there was a dream. The dream was cloudy at first, and jumbled the way dreams skip from place to place and people turn into spiders and don't make any sense, but then it became so vivid that it felt completely real. I was seeing the totality of something truly terrible: an apocalypse. The T.F.G. controlled people's bodies and minds. People were killing each other, not knowing what was going on. Children, whose minds were taken away, gradually fell into mindless submission, fulfilling whatever plan the T.F.G. had for them, even murder.

In this dream state, I also wondered if I were under the control of the T.F.G. I remembered my mom telling me that the T.F.G. controlled people's minds without the person being conscious of it, so how would I know either way? Taking away free will was like destroying a person's life; it was all just too terrible. The realistic quality of these images, this glimpse of the power of the T.F.G., this perfect picture of their ultimate goal, scared me so much that I woke up suddenly, like being dropped onto my bed from ten feet up.

I was sweating and thirsty and wanting to shake the feeling of that dream so I got out of bed and walked silently to the refrigerator. *Luckily*, I tried to reassure myself, *I have parents that won't let that happen to me.* I opened the door to the fridge with weak arms, still groggy from sleep. I took out a cup of water to refresh my dry throat. When I went to refill my cup, I heard a noise. At

26

first I thought that my stomach made the noise, but I wasn't hungry at all. So I put the glass of water back into the fridge and stood there in the dark, just listening. *Maybe this is just my imagination*, I thought, trying to steady my nerves. But then I heard the noise again. It was the sound of rustling in the bushes outside, which fit the terrifying sight of two dark images standing in the yard.

I knew I was not dreaming anymore so I searched for the closest weapon. All I could find were two huge serving spoons in the open dishwasher. *Seriously?* went through my mind as I quietly took a spoon in each of my cold trembling hands and slipped behind the kitchen island where it was especially dark. I looked back to where I saw the images and they were gone. *Are they in the house?* I knew if I screamed and ran to my parents, which was definitely my first instinct, they would kill us all. The only thing I could think to do was knock these people out with the spoons. Before I could grasp how ridiculous that idea was, something made a clunk behind me. I whipped my head around and saw them moving toward me. I could also tell that they hadn't seen me yet and that they were carrying knives in their hands. Big knives. *You've got to be kidding me*, I thought.

I crouched into the smallest ball I could make myself in the darkness and watched the two strangers' every move. They neared the kitchen with knives in hand as they stealthily walked in the direction of the master bedroom. I gripped the spoons tightly making the knuckles on my hands go white from the grip. Closer, the men looked smaller than they had as shadows in the yard, a realization that allowed some confidence to build in me. I leapt up and hurled a heavy metal spoon into the forehead of one of the two guys and he dropped like a rock, holding his ears and wailing in pain.

The unharmed man jumped at me for vengeance, but I moved away so swiftly that the man lost his balance and knocked over a stool as he staggered to his feet. I struck the guy in the side of the head with a spoon and he fell over. It was like a movie. I felt like some kind of spoon-wielding superhero. Noise engulfed the house and I prayed that my parents would wake up and help me finish them off. Just then, the other man who was hit first jumped on top of me and pinned me to the ground. I tried to throw him off but the man was too strong. I was able to let out a scream before the man covered my mouth. I pulsed all over. *I am toast.*

The man on top of me pulled out his knife and smiled that weird smile. He looked right into the eyes of this kid he was about to kill. *Me.* I struggled mightily under his weight. It was hard to breathe but I managed to get an arm free and swat away the knife. The stranger leaned to pick it up, raising himself onto his knees and giving me a chance to catch my breath. I made a move to free myself but I was too fatigued to keep the man from pinning me down again and regaining control over his knife. He then raised his knife above my body and shook a little, almost like he was trying to will himself *not* to stab me. I started to cry as I braced myself for my last moments in this world. The stranger lingered in his position. I thought maybe he was showing mercy because of my age.

Then I heard footsteps and the man on top of me became weak. At the same time I could see the tip of the knife that had just punctured the man's body. Blood came pouring from the stranger's chest and onto my shirt. I tried to move as someone

29

pulled the man off of me. The shape of another man appeared in front of me, and I winced at the thought of another attack. My eyes were blurry with tears. "John," I heard the man say. "John, are you ok?" I opened my eyes to see my dad, extending his hand to help me up.

"Dad," I cried as my dad pulled me into a hug, "I was so scared!"

My mom rushed into the room and came right over to us as my dad pushed me out and held my shoulders, looking me over for wounds. "I was scared too," he said. "Thank God I heard you." He stretched my shirt out to make sure the blood all over me wasn't mine. Satisfied it wasn't, he continued, "I don't imagine any of us are going to get any more sleep tonight, but I think you should try, John. Your mom and I will stay up and keep watch. At least lie down and close your eyes."

I would have bet a million dollars that I was not going to fall asleep again that night, but as I heard my mom and dad talking in the next room, I slipped into the deep dreamless slumber of utter exhaustion.

CHAPTER 4

The morning rays hit my face through the window and my eyes were trying to open into a squint. My body was sore, hardly prepared for the exciting day ahead. I turned onto my side so I could see my clock. I usually woke up at 7:00 a.m. and in spite of all the turmoil the night before, it was no different this morning. My body desperately wanted to sleep longer so I sat up to get rid of that urge. Cold air filled my lungs as my chest heaved in and out. I took many deep breaths. For all I knew, this would be a day of blood and death. I was terrified but I resisted the urge to jump back in bed and forget all of it. I wanted it to be a normal day but it wasn't. *A group of maniacs wants to turn our brains into obedient mush. I've got to try to stop it.*

Just as quickly as I found my courage, I lost it. *How am I supposed to stop this train? I can't control the wild, unstoppable things that make this world awful. I wish I could. I know I would if I could but how can*

I accomplish the impossible? But I pushed that voice back knowing that my parents were counting on me and not wanting me to screw it up by thinking too much. I forced my mind onto the most immediate task of finding the right clothes for quick action.

Mom and dad were preparing breakfast in the kitchen. It seemed so ordinary. I could smell my mom's savory chocolate chip pancakes from my room. I changed my clothes and grabbed my phone to call Chase. After a few seconds of ringing, Chase's voice boomed in my ear like he had a megaphone. He sounded tired, like he just awoke from a coma. "Hey, John. What's up? You excited for some shots?"

Chase was a sloth in the mornings. I could picture him trying to sound like he was ready to go while he rolled over to see what time it was on his football clock. *Man, I am going to hate myself for having to tell him the bad news.* "Dude, we can't get our shots today," I said. "I mean, we have to go get our shots, but we can't actually get our shots."

"What, are you scared of a little needle?" Chase teased.

Um, yeah, but we've got bigger problems than that, I thought. This was going to be harder to explain than I expected so I tried

32

to sound serious, which was always hard to do when I was talking to Chase. "Chase," I said, "I need you to be serious. I'm not joking."

"Fine, what is it?"

"There is this secret group. They are called the T.F.G. When you are fourteen, like us, they put a tracker into your body instead of the usual immunization. Then they can control you, and you have no idea that they are controlling you! Don't tell anybody about this, Chase, or else we are screwed, big time."

"John, you're so lame. Do you want me to give you some prank calling tips?" Chase asked, laughing at his own joke.

"I swear upon a stuffed animal from the claw machine game that I am not joking," I swore.

"That is pretty persuasive, dude. I don't know," Chase said.

"Have I ever lied to you?"

"Yes, actua—"

"Come on Chase. I called you for a reason and I am dead serious. I need your help. Meet me outside the clinic at 8:30. Don't go in without me, and don't tell your mom anything about what I've told you, even if you don't believe me. Like I said, we can't get those shots but your mom has to think you will."

"My mom? You mean, supposing you're not just making up this whole crazy story, my mom has a tracker and is being controlled by some evil mastermind?" Chase got quiet, and then laughed uncomfortably. "That actually makes a lot of sense. I suppose your folks have somehow escaped this same fate?"
Sadly, I could tell the truth was starting to sink in. "Mine, along with a few others, didn't receive their shots," I admitted.

"Hmm, well, I guess I can meet you there at 8:30," Chase agreed, "but is there some kind of *plan* for going in there and *not* getting our shots?"

Chase was definitely on board now but I couldn't explain everything to him over the phone. I just didn't have time. "Listen," I said, "that's all I can say right now. When I see you at the clinic, I'll fill you in on the rest. But whatever happens, you just can't get that shot. Got it?"

Chase let out a huge sigh and squeezed out an uncertain "Ok" before he said his mom was calling him and he had to go. The phone went silent and I started to feel anxious about the reality of this day. I wanted badly to bring Chase's parents back but we didn't yet have an antidote to this mind-destroying serum, and I didn't want him to know that. Maybe our whole plan would go off without a hitch and my parents would get into the lab and figure out how that stuff works and what can be done to counteract it. I let myself hope that we would make the world right again.

And, with that final push of blind faith I finished getting ready for what I thought might be the most important day of my life. I put my phone in my front pocket knowing I would soon need it again and I looked around my room for anything that I might need later, gathering only a few photos and tucking them into my back pocket before slowly closing the door. I then shared an amazingly normal breakfast with my parents and the three of us got into the car, barely saying a word. I turned my head as we pulled away, taking in this memory of my house just in case I would never see it again.

As we made our way to the so-called doctor's appointment, it was completely silent in the car. I decided to break the ice by asking if we were still on track with the same plan. They shot each other a quick glance and proceeded to tell me that our plan had a fatal flaw--namely, that after two sets of visitors last night, the T.F.G. had to be waiting for us and that as soon as I signed in for my appointment, it would all be over. *When were you going to break this to me?* I screamed inside my head.

"We do have a plan B," my dad offered. "When you get into the clinic, sign in as Chase and ask for the bathroom. Hopefully, they don't know one kid from another and they let you through. Tell Chase not to come in until there are a few other kids in the waiting room, and then to pretend to sign in. His name will already be on the list, of course. John, you've still got to get us into the basement but you can't go back up. Once we are in, the three of us will have to try to set off an alarm so the place is evacuated. We are still hoping there is time to test the serum but there is no guarantee. And there's no telling what they might be prepared to do to stop us. We have guns if we need them."

Guns? This plan seemed so far from reality but I feared it would be real pretty soon. *This is going to be a barmy day*, I thought. We stopped about a block from the clinic and found a parking spot on the street. The car was silent and my parents were staring straight ahead. We were all gathering strength. "John, send us a text when you get a window open, and tell us which window," my mom ordered. With that, I got out of the car and marched toward the clinic, like a soldier stepping up to the front line.

CHAPTER 5

From across the parking lot I could see Chase and his mom almost reach the front door, so I yelled, "Hey, Chase!"

"Sup?" he cried back, looking relieved to see me, and terrified at the same time. His mom gave me that fake smile and told Chase not to be long, as she headed into the clinic ahead of us. I had a fleeting thought that she was going to sign Chase in, but there were a million other things on my mind too. "What's the plan?" Chase asked, as we both peered into the glass door watching his mom.

"I'm going to sign in as you and then secretly let my parents into the building. They will test the serum in this shot and stop the T.F.G.," I declared as if this made perfect sense. "Give me a little head start and then when you come in just pretend to sign in, you know, over the spot where you're already signed in."

"It's a good thing I trust you, man, because this is beyond crazy." Chase was looking really nervous now, "So, is that it? I mean, what's the plan to stop these guys from giving *me* that shot?"

"My parents are going to set off an alarm so the building is evacuated. Don't worry," I said as confidently as I could, wondering myself how in the hell this was going to work. "Okay, I'm going in. Wait until I've gone into the back before you come in."

I walked in and heard the TV on, recognizing the voice of Dora the Explorer explaining something in Spanish. "Es malo," she declared. *You've got that right*, I replied in my head. I approached the desk with all kinds of butterflies in my stomach trying to keep my cool. The sign-in sheet was there and sure enough, Chase's mom had already signed him in. I pulled the sheet toward me and pretended to write on the page. I looked up and the receptionist was sitting behind the desk doing a crossword puzzle. *That's convenient*, I thought. "Um, excuse me. Can I use the bathroom?" I asked, trying to get her attention.

39

She glanced up and smiled at me before she got up to open the door that headed into the back. *This is going smoothly so far*, I thought as Dora went to a commercial about Cocoa Puffs. In the back, the hall was empty. I saw the bathroom immediately on the left and scanned ahead for a way to get downstairs. At the end of the hall was an unmarked door and I practically ran straight for it. It was a steel door with a small thick meshed window, and it was locked. *Es malo!* As I stood there trying to figure out what to do, I heard footsteps on metal stairs, no doubt from the basement, heading toward the other side of that door. I ran to the nearest door, hoping to hide inside. It was an empty exam room and it was open. And it had a window so I could see what was going on out in the hall. *Que suerte!* I thought, imagining I was Dora's sidekick for the day.

As the basement door swung open, and a woman in a lab coat hurriedly made her way down the hall, I realized that I'd have a chance to get in as the door was closing on one of those slowing mechanisms. The woman disappeared into the reception area and I slipped out of my hiding spot to grab the basement door knob just as it was about to slam shut. I was in! Now to find the windows in the basement and get one open. I was feeling pretty good about the way our plan was unfolding.

My lucky streak continued as I quietly made my way down the stairs and found the lab to be deserted, except for a few albino rats in cages. Suddenly, as I locked eyes with a rat, the reality of this menace started to haunt me. I thought about Chase and his parents, both controlled by the T.F.G. I felt bad for my friend. I could picture his face a little while ago in front of the clinic. He stared at his mother with deep despair and sadness, which I had never seen on his goofy face before. Still, it was easy to read his mind. He looked like he was thinking about all the conversations he could never have, all the fun times he could never experience with his mother, and how all of those dreams had been crushed by the hands of this abominable society. I could only imagine how he felt about his dad, the father he admires so much but who isn't ever there for him. Chase will never know what it feels like to be loved by his parents the way I do, all because of this diabolical population. He will never even play ball with his dad because this secret group doesn't want him to. They would rather replace those childhood moments with experimenting on innocent people and making them do whatever those bazaar bastard brains want them to do.

I was locked on those red beady eyes wondering if that rat was trying to tell me something telepathically. "Maybe we can get Chase's parents back if you'll help me," I said to the rodent as I opened his little cage door, "That would mean the world to me." As my new friend fixed his attention on his widening prospects, I set my sights on the old window just above and pried the painted-over metal clasp free. The window was also painted shut but at least it was now unlocked. I figured my parents could force it open from the outside so I grabbed my phone from my pocket and typed a text to my mom: "North, front."

While I waited for my parents to get the message and find their way to the window, my mind drifted back to the receptionist and her smile just before she let me into the back. *That stupid smile.* It's so obvious now when I meet people that are being controlled, but of course just like the T.F.G., we are idiots, always distracted on cell phones and video games. We do not think about or even realize that adults, teenagers, even our parents, are mute with our faces glued to a screen. The thought was interrupted when my screen lit up with a text from my mom: "Fire alarm. Bathroom. Hurry."

That's basically when my luck ran out. I was making my way to the bathroom upstairs for some firecracker fun, when it all fell apart. Not seconds after I heard the basement door slam behind me, a man in scrubs stepped out of an exam room, looked up from his iPad and asked me what I was doing. "I, I'm trying to find my exam room," I stumbled, "I went to the bathroom and forgot which way to go." The man seemed satisfied with my response but then he asked me for my name. I froze. *What the hell do I do now?*

"There you are, son" I heard my mom say, "Your dad and I were just getting worried about you."

What the....? They must have come in the front door and now here we were, my parents and I on our way to an exam room where I would get a shot that would erase my free will.

CHAPTER 6

A wave of nausea consumed me as I followed the fake doctor down the long hallway. My parents were right behind me probably feeling the same amount of sickness as I was. I was trembling as I walked down the long hallway. My parents could kill him right now, I thought, but that would mess up the plan, if they still had one. The walk to our room was short but it felt a lot longer. I was definitely going to be sick. The man in front of me was wearing blue scrubs and he had a pencil behind his ear. I wondered what he was feeling since he was brainwashed. Maybe he didn't feel anything. On the other hand, maybe he felt conflicted, like the man that was going to stab me at home but trembled as he seemed to be fighting his own body. We passed several identical rooms with brown doors, and each had a small window. I glanced inside the rooms and as far as I could tell all of the patients getting shots looked to be about my age.

I wished we could save them all, but I wasn't even sure we would be saving anyone at this point. I was hoping that Chase was still okay and since I didn't see him in any of the rooms, I took that to be a good sign that he had at least found some way to stall and was still okay. That was like Chase, very resourceful. I counted five rooms total before we went through a similar door on the right. The room was bright with a long patient bed, cabinets on one side, and chairs on the other. I sat on the bed and dangled my legs off the edge, wondering what the T.F.G. had programmed into the doctor's brain.

"Wait here. The doctor will be with you soon," the pencil-eared man said just before he left us, probably, I suspected, to get more patients who would soon be under the control of the T.F.G. too. Once the door finished creaking as it fully closed, I looked around for cameras but didn't see any.

My parents sat in front of me on two different chairs. They desperately wanted to explain the change in plan but I jumped off the bed and embraced my parents in a hug. I was crying and I didn't care who judged me because my parents were there. I knew if I were to lose them, I wouldn't be able to forgive

45

myself for playing it too cool. My mom started to tear up as she hugged me back, tightly, and my dad surrounded us in a great hug. That hug was the most important and most uplifting thing I had ever felt in my life. My parents, I decided right then and there, were the best thing that had ever happened to me. I wanted so much to follow through with our plan and to stop this terrible society so the rest of these teenagers and their parents could have a closeness like us.

They let go of the hug, and again it seemed like they had to tell me something urgently. I didn't let them. "Thank you so, so much for everything you have done for me," I said wiping my tears with my dark blue t-shirt. "I don't think I can move on if you guys don't make it out."

None of us knew where that idea came from, and its prophetic quality scared all of us. My mom and dad shot each other a look, and my dad seized the moment to speak. "Let's all cross our fingers for the best possible outcome today. Right now the most pressing issue is quietly getting you and Chase out of here without getting your shots. We have to think on our feet. This is a fluid situation now." My dad looked worried as he gave us another important hug. As we each stepped back from our embrace, our minds were like one in that moment. "I love you." I said. "We love you too," replied my parents. There was nothing left to say. Nothing that mattered anyway. I turned around and hopped back on the bed, with my legs dangling from the side of it. My parents sat back down in their chairs and readied themselves.

Hardly a second passed, though it felt like an hour, when the door opened. This time, it was the doctor. "Good morning," he said to us as he approached the counter next to me. I nodded casually in agreement even though I thought it was not a good morning. My parents responded with an appropriate, "Good morning." My family looked completely normal as if we didn't just bawl our eyes out. The doctor set some paperwork down on the counter next to me. He noticed me staring at him nervously so he said, "Don't worry kid, it will be over in a flash." He smiled and then looked back at his forms. *It will be over in a bad flash for you*, I thought. The man looked up from the paper and then asked, "John, is it?" "Yes," I answered.

The doctor pulled a pen out of his shirt pocket and started writing some notes on the papers spread across the counter in front of him. My parents looked extremely nervous. To break the silence my mom said, "So what is going to happen today?" The doctor looked at her casually and said, "Your son, John, will receive his fourteen-year-old shots. The shots will only make sure that he doesn't become very sick when he is older." The doctor held a concerned look with my mom before returning to the paperwork. *Does he think the T.F.G. is controlling my mom too or does he know it's us and he's stalling until the T.F.G. come in here to kill us?* It looked like my parents were wondering the same thing.

A few more seconds passed and the doctor caught me shaking. "It's just one little shot. No need to be frightened," he said, which under the circumstances was not very reassuring. I nodded my head and stopped fidgeting with my thumbs. The doctor tucked the papers into their file, picked up a needle, and turned his back to us while he filled the syringe with the brainwashing serum. Then he turned to me and said, "I am going to inject you with the good and healthy medicine I told you about. I am going to put it in the side of your neck so hold still. This will only take a second." That was it. I was freaking out inside. As he put his arm up I knew I had to make a move. I hit the middle of his arm and he dropped the needle. He clutched his injured arm and yelled, "What the…" Before he could finish cursing my dad inserted the needle into the doctor's neck.

The doctor's face turned pale like a ghost and then it went back to normal. "Please sit down," my dad whispered into his ear in a calm voice. The doctor obeyed as if he was hypnotized.

"Great work," my mom said excitedly, "I didn't expect that to happen. Does this stuff allow anyone to control anyone?"

My dad seemed just as puzzled and decided to test the theory. We walked to the door and my dad said to the doctor, "Turn around so that you can stare at the wall. Don't move a muscle or else you lose the game of freeze. And you don't want to lose the game of freeze." The doctor did exactly what my dad said. Once the doctor completed his 180 degree turn and faced the wall, he sat there completely motionless. I thought it was so cool that my dad could command an adult to play a kid's game and force him to go into "timeout." My mom didn't need any more evidence. She opened up her enormous purse and gave my dad a pistol and a hand grenade. Then she pulled out a weapon of her own. It looked like a gun Unbox Therapy would do a review on.

Every nook and cranny of this beast had an attachment of some sort that would scare the heck out of anyone. I almost laughed at the sight of them. My dad's small plain pistol was perfectly suited for his calm personality while my mom's futuristic 2S72 showed off her creative character. It was like the way she always picked the craziest and best gift at white elephant exchanges. My train of thought went off the rails as the doctor started mumbling to himself.

"We are watching you," my dad said sternly. "Don't move a bit. Even if you hear a door opening or gunshots, don't turn around. You want to win the freeze game, right?"

My mom elbowed my dad in the side, "Don't tell him everything!"

"What do we do now?" I asked. I was shivering from being in this cold room and I was anxious to find Chase before it was too late.

My dad read my mind, "I'm going to check the hall and when it's clear you are going to find your friend and we are going to get you both out of here somehow." My dad opened the door, a little at first and then all the way, and we peered out into the hallway. Chase could be in any of these rooms so I would have to check them all, trying not to be seen.

"It's looking more and more like we're going to have to use these things," my mom said, referring to the weapons that she had stashed in her purse until now. "If so, we will meet you and Chase outside where we dropped you off this morning. It's only a block away. Go there as quickly as you can."

"Ok. See ya soon," I said.

"Hopefully," my mom replied, holding onto my hand a little too long. I pleaded for this to not be the last time I saw them. I looked into her eyes, and then my dad's, and I knew I had a job to do. I let go of my mom's hand and silently ran down the left side of the hallway. I looked through the small windows of the doors looking for Chase. I first saw a family with twins who had just gotten their shots, then a family with one girl who were still waiting for the doctor. *He has to be here,* I thought in my head. After a few more rooms I finally spotted Chase. I was standing outside of his room when I saw the doctor fill the syringe with the fake medicine. I trembled not knowing what to do as the doctor raised the needle to Chase's neck. Chase spotted me and mouthed

51

the words, "What do I do?" I lifted my hand to the doorknob and burst in.

The doctor stopped moving as he looked at me in the doorway. "Uh, hi," I said while practically peeing my pants. He put the needle down and stared at me for what seemed like a long time. "You are not vaccinated, are you?" the doctor asked as he picked up the needle he had just set down. I tried to run but I couldn't move. It was as if someone else took over my body. I tried to push my arms outwards but my body rejected the movement. The doctor could see how scared I was and he calmly walked towards me with the brainwashing shot. Every step he took felt like a step closer to my death until a loud gunshot rang and the doctor dropped to the ground. I managed to look behind me to see my parents. My dad's pistol was smoking at the tip.

CHAPTER 7

I stared at both of them, trying to get my head around my dad being this killing machine all of a sudden. *That's five guys in less than 24 hours.* I was speechless. Chase, on the other hand, was acting like a man on death row that just got pardoned. "Thank you so much!" Chase said, moving away from the corpse in the middle of the room, "That was a close call." Chase awkwardly shook my dad's hand and then hugged him, and my dad awkwardly hugged him back.

"Alrighty. Now, we need to get out of here before reinforcements arrive," my dad said, just as the faint sound of approaching sirens could be heard outside. We peered through the high window in the exam room as the dreadful noise got louder and we saw a dark van screech to a halt near the front entrance. Right away soldiers loaded with guns and other accessories jumped out of the car and started running towards the entrance.

There was no time to think because they were so fast and almost upon us.

"Hide now!" my mom screamed, "Get cover and your dad and I will take care of them. Don't forget, we have the element of surprise, so hide!" My parents then bolted out of the room and disappeared down the hall.

The sirens were so loud that I could barely hear what my mom said but I immediately looked around for a place to hide. "Remember lockdowns?" I asked Chase. "Let's hide in one of the rooms and close the blinds and turn the lights out like in a lockdown. It might work better than staying under a desk or chair. Follow me." I told Chase and before he could say anything sprinted toward a room I passed earlier. We opened the door and inside was a girl about our age. The girl turned to us and yelled, "What the heck is going on?" She seemed scared. I figured she didn't get her shot yet because usually a nice brainwashed robot doesn't yell at you when you open a door.

"Shhhh," I whispered. I closed the blinds as Chase turned off the lights. Out of nowhere I felt hands on my back and then something pulling me backwards and I hit the floor with a bang. I grunted as the girl pinned me down to the floor.

"I'm not letting you go anywhere until you tell me what's going on," she said in a mean voice, "And if your friend tries to save you, which he won't because he isn't smart and tough enough to do anything, I'll punch you so hard in the eye that you won't be able to see for weeks."

"Hey! I only have one 'C' and that's in math class!" Chase said, sounding hurt.

The girl ignored Chase and pushed me down even harder. "Ok fine, just chill," I grunted. "There is a secret government who tracks and controls us when we get our fourteen-year-old vaccine shots. Instead of a positive vaccine they put this brain-washing virus and tracker into us. So to cut it short, almost everybody over fourteen is a robot controlled by the secret government called the T.F.G. and now they are trying to kill us because we know this. So if you want to live, you can let me go and help us take them down."

Yeah, like she's going to believe that, I thought as she loosened her grip on me. I stood up and moved my shoulders and legs to get some blood running through them again. She was still squatting where she had me pinned and started to ramble. "I guess I have no choice but to trust you," she said. "It kind of makes sense knowing that my parents and other adults barely talk and instead just smile awkwardly. I will join you guys but if anything seems a little off I *will* turn you in. Besides, my parents won't notice anyway if I leave them. They never say hello or goodbye when I come or leave home. Sorry I was tough on you. I just had no idea why two funny looking dudes turned off the lights and closed the blinds in here."

"I'm sorry. You're right. I should have said something to you when we came in," I told her. "I'm sorry you had to find out about your parents this way."

"Thanks," she said, standing up from her position of despair.

"Um guys, I hate to break up the Hallmark moment here but I just heard some glass shatter and some bullets fly by. No biggie though," Chase exclaimed.

"Alright let's get out of here," I said.

I looked through the narrow window of our door and saw my parents fighting off the T.F.G.'s SWAT team. *Who are these people?* I wondered proudly. I then noticed that the back of my dad's green shirt was dark--like blood, not sweat. I needed to help him but they told us to hide. My mom appeared untouched, luckily. I turned around to see Chase and the girl waiting for a response from me about what was going on. "Alright, my parents are barely holding back the T.F.G. soldiers, so that means we have to act fast and find an exit to get out of here, and it would be great if we can bring my parents with us. Any suggestions on where we can leave?" I looked at them while trying to answer the question myself.

"Maybe we could fit through that vent over there by the bed," Chase suggested.

I went over to the vent Chase pointed at and they both followed me. I pulled on the cage that closed the vent off. It was very firmly sealed and even with all my muscle I couldn't budge it. My neck was bulging and if I didn't stop I may have passed out from the loud ringing gunshots and the strain I was putting on my body. "I can't take this cap off," I said, catching my breath.

"I got it," Chase said coming up to the vent. He tugged and pulled it in many ways but still no progress was made.

"Let me try aga…" I started to say as I was interrupted by the girl who had been watching us the whole time.

"Wow, you guys are quite the comedy team. How long were you going to try before you noticed that the vent is way too small for us and your parents to fit through? This is no movie," she said glaring back and forth between the two of us. She then stepped up to the vent and slid her hand along the left side of it. She flipped a switch there and the cage of the dark vent clicked open. "This is new technology, folks! It's called, a *lock*," she said in the most adorably patronizing way. Chase and I stood there with our jaws dropped.

"Thanks, Houdini. Why didn't you tell us in the first place? We really don't have time for this," Chase said in a sarcastic scolding tone.

"You're welcome," she replied in kind, "I think we need a new exit though."

I thought for a second remembering how I got into my house during yesterday's break in. "Hey listen up," I said. They came over hoping I had a solution. "Yesterday when my parents were captured I used the back door of my house to get in. If we can get to the back door then we may have a chance. If no one is back there waiting for us, I mean."

They looked at me and nodded. "It's all we've got. Let's do this," Chase said.

We opened the door and immediately ran to the wall ahead of us for cover. To the left of us were loud pops coming from the lobby. There was another hallway that was indistinguishable from the hallway we were in except for a crevice I noticed earlier when I was looking for the door to the basement. I couldn't quite make out signage nearby because bullets were whizzing by. The walls around us were pocked from bullets, and there were shells on the floor everywhere. In order to get across we would need my parents to use full force and stop all the bullets from coming through here.

"Mom," I yelled, "we need you to cover us for a few seconds." I could tell she heard me because she started talking to my dad who was still bleeding across his back. I turned around to see Chase and the girl waiting for me to make a move. The girl looked calm and determined, unlike Chase who was obviously scared to death. "I am pretty sure my parents can cover us so we can get over to the other side," I shouted to them. I pointed to the crevice and said, "See that little indent over there? I think that might lead to the back door so we need to get over there." They nodded in agreement and when I peeked out toward my parent's location trying not to get hit by flying bullets, I heard my mom yell, "three seconds!"

A loud boom shook the whole building. It was one of the grenades my mom had smuggled in here in her purse. "That's the signal," I shouted. I sprinted across the hall with my friends following. We made it to the other end of the hallway safely. *It's not everyday you get to escape a war zone*, I thought. Now I could see that the crevice was a narrow hallway with vials of serum lined up on shelves on both sides. At the end of this hallway I could see a door. "Let me go and see if the door is unlocked and if it's clear outside," I told my friends.

"Be careful," Chase said with genuine concern as I ran through the hallway ignoring the containers of blue liquid on either side of me. I reached the door and looked through the small peep hole. On the other side of the door I saw a few T.F.G. soldiers talking to each other. There were only five of them, unless there were more out of sight. They had long guns resting in their arms but they were way less armed than the SWAT team inside the building. I had to check if the door was unlocked so I rested my hand on the door handle and twisted it slightly. Luckily the guards were lost in their conversation and didn't notice as I pushed slightly against the door and it creaked open a few millimeters. I let the door close as slowly and carefully as I could and I crouched down by the door thinking about what to do now.

I had an idea. I raced back through the serum-filled hallway to my friends. My heart almost stopped when I saw that my parents had made their way through the battlefield and were crouched there too with Chase and the girl. My mom looked terrible with black smears on her face but my dad looked worse. In the midst of this warzone, he was bleeding and she was crying because the husband that she knew most of her life may die trying to protect us. "Hey mom," I said to her softly, part of me knowing that this was not going to end well. She put down her gun and hugged me and then said, "Hey my little Johnny."

Chase brought us back to the warzone, asking, "So what are we going to do now? Make a run for it?"

"The back door is unlocked but there are five T.F.G. guards outside," I tried to tell them over the sound of more gunfire.

"You have got to be kidding me," the girl said, airing the frustration we were all feeling about this continuous run of bad luck.

"Well, out the back looks better than out the front," I said, trying to sound optimistic. "At least we have a chance that way. But we can't get past those guards without your help taking them out," I said, looking at my mom and dad.

"I'm already hurt and bleeding," my dad said faintly, "I won't make it because I can't feel my back at all. I can try to hold off the guards for you on this side, even if it's the last thing I do."

My mom squeezed her eyes and tears came out in buckets as she held my dad's face in her hands for a moment and kissed him. Then she picked up her gun and ran toward the door. "John," she commanded, "when you're ready, kick that door open and follow me out."

I looked back at Chase and the girl. "Ready?" I asked them. "Sure," the girl replied. Chase nodded like usual.

"Get the hell out of here," my dad hollered as he threw himself into the hallway firing his gun like a madman.

"Now," I yelled as I kicked the door open. My mom ran in front of me and shot at the guards. Bullet after bullet, the men dropped like flies. *Mom could be in one of those slow-motion first person shooting games and have the number one leading score*, I thought, pushing away the image of my dad giving up everything to save us back there.

We were running away from the fake clinic and the flying bullets and the dead T.F.G. guards when my mom suddenly stopped. "John, you need to get far away from here and find a place to lay low for a while. I brought some money with me so that we could rent a place to stay," she said while setting her gun down. She reached into her pocket and pulled out a worn brown leather wallet. When I took the wallet, my fingers brushed over the round emblem filled with maze-like patterns, including various shaped circles. "I am giving this to you so that in case anything happens to me at least you will have it. You need to keep it safe. It has some important things in it," she said as she handed me the wallet.

I took the wallet and put it in my pocket. "Mom," I said, "stay with us! Where are we going to go? How are we going to survive? Who can we trust?" But I knew she had to go back for my dad, just as I knew that Chase, this girl, and I would have to find our way alone. My mom picked up her gun, ran toward the building and disappeared through the back door, and we looked around for a way to run.

"See that path down over there," the girl said as she pointed to a gravel walkway with trees on both sides of it. "That's where we can go." The back of the doctor's office was surrounded by trees and grass but was close to some main streets. It was relatively quiet back here but you could still hear the sound of gunfire in the building. "Let's go then," I said, trying hard to stay focused on what we had to do, hoping against hope that my parents would somehow survive this and find me. We headed for the path but then stopped as we heard more T.F.G. sirens getting closer, and then a massive explosion.

The building behind us was engulfed in flames and I reeled around to take in the most terrible thing I had ever seen. I fell to the ground feeling faint. "Mom!" I screamed at the top of my lungs. I lost all sense of what was going on and tears welled up in my eyes. Another T.F.G. van speeding to the scene went right past us but I didn't care because I knew my parents were dead. Chase and the girl were pulling me back, but I broke through their pull and ran toward the building. The heat was intense and I fell to my knees, pounding the concrete with my fist, sobbing. "Mom," I screamed, "I'm so sorry. I'm so sorry. I'm so sorry."

I'm not sure how long I was like this but I looked up to see my friends staring at me in a daze. "I'm so sorry, John. But we have to leave *now*," Chase said. Chase and the girl helped lift me up from the ground. I stared at the inferno, the warzone, the clinic, my parent's coffin. I was speechless. I had mixed emotions of rage and sadness in my head and heart and I had no idea what to feel. This was all happening way too fast. The girl broke my thoughts by reminding me that the T.F.G. will kill us next if we don't get out of here. I looked back at my only family for the last

CHAPTER 8

I turned around and took a deep breath. We started walking away from the disaster. Our walk turned into a jog and then a full sprint. The landscape became a green blur. None of us talked for a good few minutes. We all felt the same thing: loss. "Let's focus on the future and not the past," I said as we slowed down. "Some people say to wait on making decisions, to cross the bridge when you get there, but I think we should start planning ahead."

"You're right," the girl said. "Hey, I never fully introduced myself. I'm Hazel."

"I'm John and this doofus is Chase," I said as Chase picked up his hand in a half-wave. "It's almost noon and we need to find a place to live before it gets dark. I know that once we reach Amber, there are some dilapitated apartments and condos we could choose from." I thought about all those drives we took through Amber when I was a kid and how useful they would be now. I felt myself tearing up and I stopped in my tracks. "Hang on a second, guys."

Chase and Hazel stopped too and we sat down on a little hill under some trees. "What now?" Chase said. He looked ridiculously tired. I pulled out the wallet my mom gave me and opened it. Inside was a thick wad of cash. All 50s and 100s. I showed the bills to my friends and they both looked stunned. None of us had ever seen that much money before.

"Sweet," Chase said, downplaying his sudden exuberance.

"We won't be using that on sweets though," Hazel joked dryly. She seemed to always have a retort like that, which I guessed was the verbal equivalent of physically pinning someone down to get answers.

"Of course not," I replied as Chase drooped his head like a disappointed dog. I put the money back in the wallet and looked around for anything else my mom placed in it. There were a few pictures that I would save for other desperate times. There was also a jump drive which I pulled out and showed my friends.

"Looks like we need to get a laptop besides an apartment," I told them.

As I closed the leather wallet, I noticed again the cool circular shape embedded on the top of it. I traced the pattern with my finger thinking about how much I loved new starts and turning over new leaves. But my heart felt sick. *Next time I turn over a new leaf, I want it to be a happy change instead of being homesick forever.* "We are almost at the city of Amber so let's keep going," I said, trying to erase thoughts of my parents from my mind.

We came down from the hill and started running again. Since it was hot outside and it was the middle of the day, there weren't too many people on the path. In no time we made it to the outskirts of Amber. The city was circular with trees and mountains surrounding and protecting it. Streets meandered through the city and suddenly changed names, making it easy to get lost. Buildings, stores, and houses of many types flowed through the city. It wasn't the worst place you could live, my mom had told me. People here were mostly quiet and happy and caused no trouble. "Let's look into renting an apartment," I said as we turned onto Center Street and headed toward the heart of the city.

"Where should we start?" Hazel asked.

"There," Chase said, pointing to a huge sign hovering over a flat-roofed building that needed paint. The sign pictured a smiling bald man standing next to a sign of a smiling bald man in a yard and it said, "Ask Hester, Amber's Top Real Estate Guy."

"Seriously?" I asked laughing.

"What else do you want me to look for?" Chase replied.

"Good point," I responded. We all crossed the queerly quiet road and made our way to the building. We opened the door and were greeted with sale signs and advertisements everywhere. The store was pretty small compared to stores in my old neighborhood.

"Hello! Welcome to Hester the Real Estate Guy. My name is Hester, how may I help you?" Chase and I were struggling against an all-out crack-up. I was wondering if this guy does all the jobs at his business. I'm sure Chase was thinking the same thing. Hazel warded off the fallout from our stupidity and quickly got to the point: "We would like to rent an apartment please."

He sized us up, one by one, and I thought for sure he was going to tell us to get lost. "Yes, yes, I have many apartment options," Hester replied in a happy tone as he tightened his tie. "Let's whittle this down a little. What amenities are you looking for?"

We looked at each other in disbelief. *Amenities? How about a pool? Maybe a game room?*

"Can we see the cheapest apartment you have for rent?" Hazel broke in before I could finish my mental wish list.

"Sure, sure," the real estate guy said giddily. He clicked around his computer and then turned his monitor around so that a series of photos faced us. Chase and I tried to focus on what he was showing us. "You like it, huh?" Hester said immediately, like he just drank five shots of espresso. The pictures were amazing. It was a whole house and it seemed huge. "This rental house is good for you. It has three bedrooms and one bathroom and it's $800 a month," he said. Chase and I tried to hold in our own giddiness. I wanted to fall to the floor in tears of joy. *Man this real estate agent is the best.*

"It sounds reasonable. Where is it located?" Hazel asked him, pretending that she didn't know us.

"It's on the north side of town, right up against the forest. You'll love it." Hester replied.

It all seemed too good to be true but we needed a place, and this was a place. "That sounds wonderful for tourists like us," Hazel happily responded. "We will take it!"

Hester then slid a clipboard in front of Hazel, who was clearly in charge, she filled out the forms and just like that, we were out the door and on our way to our new home.

"That was too easy," I said. "Any chance that guy is with the T.F.G. and just sent us to an ambush?"

"I don't know," Chase shrugged, "maybe some of them are nice. I can see this guy renting cool houses for hardly any money to orphaned teenagers out of the goodness of his programmed heart. I think Hester is a Tracker for Good," he finished with a laugh.

My blood started to boil and I grabbed Chase by the shirt. "Don't you ever say they are nice or good, or else I will grab you again and punch the crap out of you. They murdered my family and Hazel's. You think that's no big deal? Maybe your parents are still alive but that doesn't mean you can make fun that ours aren't."

"Wow, chill. I wasn't making fun of your family," Chase said, trying to release my grip on him.

"Then why do you think this mad society that kills people we love is nice, huh?" I shot back.

"You are going crazy. You think I'm seriously making fun of you and your perfect family?" Chase yelled as he pushed me away from him.

"Oh bring it on," I told him, ready to fight. I was about to throw a punch when Hazel stepped between us.

"What is wrong with you guys? A minute ago you were laughing your butts off about some stupid guy and now you are picking a fight with each other over the same guy. Come on. We can't do this. We are a team. Now kiss and make up." Hazel put a hand on each of our shoulders and pushed us together.

"Pucker up," Chase said, which I ignored, still fuming. But of course I knew fighting wouldn't get us anywhere. I stuck out my hand as an olive branch and apologized. And Chase did the same.

"Am I not with the two most idiotic idiots in the world?" Hazel said, rolling her blue eyes. "Let's get back to what we need to do. I don't know about you guys, but I'm starving. Do you want to go out to eat or order a pizza? I saw a restaurant back there. Want to try it?"

"Sure," Chase said. In all the time I knew him, he never turned down an offer to eat.

"Yeah, let's try it," I agreed, and we headed back the way we came until Hazel spotted the restaurant she saw earlier. We entered a room full of appealing smells. We sat down and were quiet while we surveyed our menus. I decided on a double cheese burger the size of my face with a side of fries and a large fountain drink. Chase and Hazel wanted their own pizzas. I was really glad we had so much money.

I noticed how the real estate agent talked more to us than the workers in the restaurant, which gave us a chance to discuss our plans for what we were going to do in the days yet to come. "Tomorrow we need to find a store to buy a laptop so we can see what's on the jump drive," I declared as I chomped down on my burger.

"Do you want us to come with you?" Hazel asked as she was slowly conquering her pizza. "I think we should always stick together when we can just in case we get into any trouble with the T.F.G."

"Speaking of trouble, should we get weapons or anything?" Chase offered.

"For once you are a genius," I said as I reached over and high-fived him with my ketchup covered hand. Ketchup splattered onto Hazel and speckled her face. She wiped it off angrily.

"Sorry," Chase and I said in unison. Hazel rolled her eyes so I tried to change the mood: "What do you think the interior of the house *really* looks like?" I said, noting my suspicion that Hester pulled the old bait and switch on us.

"I don't care if the rooms are pretty small. I don't even care if the bathroom is small. But the kitchen must be gigantic and clean," Hazel said as a joke, as if she could do anything about it now. *This girl digs kitchens?* I wondered to myself. We kept talking about the apartment as we finished our food, realizing that no matter what it was like, we were going to need to do some shopping. I finished first and wiped up all the ketchup splatter

75

while Chase scarfed his last slice of pepperoni pizza. Hazel wrapped up her last piece of mushroom pizza in a napkin to take home.

Home? "You guys ready to go check out our new house?" I somehow choked out.

"So ready," Chase said.

We walked a couple of miles from the restaurant to the north side of the city. We saw our rental house come into view. It looked even better in person with a nice wooden porch to top it off. We had no neighbors in sight which I thought was good for safety reasons. Only woods surrounded our house. We all took the first few steps up on our porch and turned around to see the view. It was a beautiful sight full with color and light from all directions. "Wow, that's amazing," Hazel said.

"I know, right?" I said looking at the view. *The inside must be a total dump,* I thought.

I couldn't stop looking at the view. The sky was a great mixture of red, orange, blue, and grey and I stayed to watch it with Chase and Hazel until the sun went all the way down and the sky lost its color. "Ready to check out our new home?" I asked, finally looking away from the sky and the city.

I opened the door and was greeted with a pretty nice layout and furniture. In front of us there was the kitchen with an island and bar stools, cabinets along the wall, and a fridge. I turned to see Hazel nodding in approval. I didn't know why I felt a chill but I was definitely glad to see Hazel smile. Chase immediately opened the fridge to see if anything was in it, but he was met with nothing but cold air. "This place is cool," Chase said, not the least bit disappointed in the empty fridge.

"We haven't seen most of it yet," said Hazel. So we all pivoted right and stood facing the family room. It had an old TV and a few chairs gathered around it. Down the hallway was a good-sized bathroom on the left and three bedrooms clustered together.

"This one's mine," I called out as I ran into the room on the right. Hazel took the room in the middle and Chase took the one on the left. The rooms were identical with a wooden bed, a nightstand next to it with an alarm clock, and a closet. The rooms weren't fancy like they would be in a nice hotel but they were suitable for us. They even had sheets and pillows. "I am going to bed right away and when I wake up tomorrow, the first thing I am going to do is get some clothing that smells good. Are you both with me?" I called out loud enough for them to hear me from their rooms.

"You bet," Chase said at the same time Hazel yelled, "Yeah," the way someone says that when they mean that they can't wait. Since their parents were brainwashed by the T.F.G., I was pretty positive that Chase and Hazel didn't get a lot of kid-perks like I did. I was excited about changing their lives, which I thought about as I took off my shoes and shirt and placed them next to my bed. When I hopped into my cozy bed and pulled the blanket over me, thoughts about what was the craziest and saddest and most exciting day of my life raced through my head. My parents were gone and I ached as I tried to move them to the back of my mind. I tried to think about what the future was going to bring, but I was scared and nervous. I wanted to stop thinking entirely and go to sleep. "Night," I called out into the quiet house. They each responded in kind and I relaxed my body. I finally fell asleep, thinking how lucky I was for this new family and our new

home.

CHAPTER 9

As soon as I fell asleep I woke back up again. I tried to push myself off my bed but I couldn't because some weight was pulling my hands down. I tried to make myself snap back to reality from my dream-state so that I could focus on what was holding my arms down. I looked at my hands and saw metal cuffs around my wrists holding me to rods on the bed. *Where am I? What happened?* I looked around in bewilderment and saw people pulling my bed. As the image became more focused, I saw one man at every corner of the bed. They all wore identical clothing: dark black vests and beige jeans. They appeared to be soldiers.

"What is going on?" I yelled, tugging against the restraints around my arms. I tried to pull my feet up but they too were held down by metal cuffs. None of the soldiers responded to my question and we kept moving down a hallway. The hallway was illuminated by bright lights every few feet along the ceiling. "What is going on?" I yelled at them again. They continued to ignore me

so I spit at the soldier closest to my face. "Hey earless guy," I

screamed, "answer my...."

He shut me up with a punch to my face which I was

powerless to stop. My head slammed against the moving metal

bed which I suddenly realized was not the bed I fell asleep in. At

first I couldn't feel anything on the right side of my face or on the

back of my head. I tried to lift my head but pain shot through my

whole face like buckshot. I rolled my eyes around and could see

that the soldiers were still pulling the bed as if nothing happened.

I couldn't make out any more details of my predicament since my

right eye was swollen shut.

I opened my mouth to yell at him for hitting a kid but

when I moved my jaw, pain worse than before expanded across

my cheek. The only thing I could get out was a mutter: "Where

are you taking me?"

The guy I spit on looked down at me with a grin on his

face. "You'll see," he said. I set my head back on the firm

platform and thought about the terrible timing of this kidnapping.

This can't happen to me right now. I stared back up at the lights that came and went on the ceiling and decided not to try any imbecilic moves that would get me in trouble.

I groaned as the pain on the side of my face got worse. I moved my mouth around to see if I could loosen it up but that caused even more agony. My right eye was able to focus more. In fact, I noticed my eye healing faster by the second. So many questions were roaming in my head yearning for answers. "Why are you taking me away from my friends?" I asked in a more amiable voice than before.

"That will be answered when you meet him," said the soldier.

Anger and frustration were choking me. "Who's 'him'?" I asked, trying to ease my emotions and my pain.

"You will know who he is when you see him," the soldier responded, annoying me to the nth degree.

"You better answer my simple questions," I threatened, "or else when I get out of these restraints I will make sure you feel the same pain I feel right now!" It took all the strength left in me to say this.

"You stupid kid," I heard the guy to my right say. I then felt a crushing pain in my stomach as he clobbered me again. I coughed up some blood on my bare chest.

The bed stopped moving. I could barely find the strength to lift up my head to see the three other soldiers surround the guy who hit me. At first there was yelling and then a scuffle ensued as they moved away from the bed. They were clearly not focused on me anymore, or what they were supposed to be doing with me. I seized the moment to look for any possible way to get out of the cuffs. I tried to feel around with my hands as far as they would go until the restraints stopped them. With my right hand I felt a loose screw on the side of the bed that held metal pieces together.

I twisted it out with my fingers. It was like opening a tiny door knob and the screw popped right off into my hand. I then took the screw so that the flat end of it was held between my fingers and the sharp end of it was pointed away from my hand. I turned my wrist around and bent it as best as I could so that I could try to unhinge the wrist cuffs. I found the small circular slot in the cuffs for a key. I pushed the screw in the slot and it barely fit. I twisted the screw to unlock it and the screw caught on the lock's wedges. I heard a click come from the cuff and I pulled up on it as it slid open.

I glanced to my right where the soldiers were deep in their philosophical argument about whether or not you should hit a kid. It seemed like this could not go on much longer so I lifted my free arm up and moved it around to get some feeling back into it and quickly unlocked the cuff on my left hand. I then hoisted myself up against the excruciating pain in my stomach, reached over my legs and quickly undid the locks on my feet.

I looked around and saw a door not too far away behind me and an endless hallway in front of me. If I wanted to get out of here I needed to move, and soon. I knew if I ran to the door they would see me so I was left with one option. I looked down the long corridor for a way to leave unnoticed and it didn't look good. But I pushed my broken body off the bed anyway and crouched as low as I could next to it so that the soldiers would not see me. The pain in my stomach was unbearable as I maneuvered off the bed and I had to just stop there gritting my teeth before I could move again.

I tried to focus on escape routes but the pain was too intense. Luckily the metal bed had a lower platform, a shelf, that hovered between the bed and the wheels. The platform was meant to be used for small items but I had no other choice so I slid myself onto it. I put my back against the platform and lay there as still as I could, hoping that when the soldiers finished their argument they would have no idea where I went.

I closed my eyes because it helped me focus on what the soldiers were saying. Still, I only heard snippets. "…report you to Crofar if you go into a rage like that again," I heard one of the guys say. I could tell he was talking to the soldier who bluntly fired punches at me. "You better listen to what we are saying, soldier, or Crofar will give you a reason to not do it again," a different voice said this time. *Crofar? Who is Crofar?* I thought, perplexed with ever more questions.

"Ok fine I get it. Back off of me, would you. That kid is just an idiot. He's cuffed to a table and mouthing off like he's gonna make trouble. Who does he think he is?" I heard the soldier say, which made me clench my fingers into a tight fist. If I could have seen my knuckles, I would have bet they were white. I wanted to punch that guy like I have never wanted to punch anyone.

"Hey, we shouldn't be talking about Crofar in front of him. He doesn't know who we are," I could hear another soldier say in a hushed tone.

"Are you kidding me? I'll bet he's unconscious by now. He could barely see after the first punch, which he deservedly received. I mean look at him," the soldier said, turning around and pointing to the bed where I used to be.

"What the hell?" a different soldier muttered. I knew they were looking straight at the bed so I held my breath and tried to be perfectly still. I must have held my breath too long because the whole room started to fizzle around me into a dark and hollow space. Forms and voices completely disappeared. When I came to, I was back in my bedroom. I looked around me startled at the change of scenery. *Was that only a dream?*

CHAPTER 10

Almost involuntarily I thrust my torso into a sitting position on my bed, staring in a daze ahead of me. My whole body was sweating in its haste to cool itself down. I felt like a wreck. Although it was just a nightmare, it felt so real. I started to wonder if my nightmare could actually be a vision of some sort, or worse, it actually happened. But that would just be crazy and impossible. I leaned to the right to see the time and I felt some aches and pains in my stomach, which I disregarded as caused by all the bullet dodging the day before.

I looked at the clock--it was 8:00 a.m.--and I realized that this was the first night I had more than five hours of sleep in a few days. I stretched my arms above me to trickle some energy back into them. They felt so weak. I looked at my blankets all crinkled around me from my movements during the night. I threw the covers away from me so that the air swirling around me could reach my skin. I forced my stiff legs over the side of the bed, and started putting on the same shirt and socks I wore yesterday. I could not wait to go out and get some fresh clothes. I ran my hands through my dark brown hair so that it wouldn't look so messy in front of my friends. The room was still a little dark from the closed shades but it was light enough to see that my door was closed and locked.

I walked over drowsily to the door and then made my way through the dim house to the kitchen and turned on the light. I felt like I was suddenly on stage, like I was in one of my old school productions melting under blazing lights. I looked around and it appeared that I was the only one up, which was kind of surprising, but then I noticed a yellow sticky note hanging on the fridge so I walked over to read it. I immediately recognized Chase's handwriting:

Good morning! I hope you had an awesome night! Well guess what? Since you are the first one up, you can go to the grocery store and get some food so that my stomach can be full when I wake up. Look at you, doing chores on the first day. You're so kind. Also, from now on, whoever wakes up first gets to make everybody else's breakfast. Isn't that a brilliant idea? Wow, I deserve a pat on the back for that idea as well as additional time to sleep-in. Now, go do your chore and hopefully I am not the one to wake up first. Also, while you're at the store, I would love some pudding and some strawberry pie. Buy some, I mean buy as much as you can afford.

--Sir Lancelot

I chuckled to myself. I hoped I would stop having T.F.G. dreams or else I would be the one making them both breakfast for a long time. I went back to my room for my mom's wallet, turned off the kitchen light, and headed out the front door to breathe in the air of Amber City. As I exited the house, I closed the door quietly behind me and made my way to the grocery store, which was not far. The store clerks were very cordial and the store contained every edible item I could imagine. I bought boxes of pancakes, syrup, butter, puddings, drinks, yogurt, milk, plastic utensils, and an enticing strawberry pie for "Sir Lancelot."

I returned in a more energetic mood than when I left since I had had a chance to stretch my body and clear my mind from that awful nightmare. *Thank you, Chase!* I reached our home and rested the bags on the ground so that I could open the door. I fully expected Chase and Hazel to be up but when I opened the door I was welcomed back into darkness and stillness. I picked up the bags and started towards the kitchen where I laid all the groceries out on the counter and looked for shades to open to brighten up the place without turning on that ridiculous light. Once I flooded the house with sunlight, I scouted out proper places inside the fridge and cabinets for all our food.

Pancakes seemed like a perfect start to our new life so I held out the pancake mix and found the pan. I was going to make these as quietly as possible so I could surprise them with breakfast when my lazy friends finally woke up. I mixed up the batter and I transferred it to the pan in little round spreading piles. I waited for the dry bubbles to appear and flipped the cakes with a spatula, just like my mom used to. They were looking golden and delicious and I was getting anxious to see my friends' faces light up in anticipation of this feast. I continued the steps until all the batter was gone and placed them in the oven so they wouldn't get cold.

I set the table and got the syrup and butter out of the fridge. Only one thing left to do. I turned back to the oven to get the pancakes when some movement caught my attention. I turned around before I reached the pancakes and there was Chase sitting at the table already, with fork and knife in hand. "What are you waiting for? Bring me some pancakes!" Chase barked at me like a youngster beckoning for ice cream.

"No 'thank you' or 'please'?" I asked.

"Are you really going to parent me?" he said, with that goofy smirk on his face. I rolled my eyes at Chase's reply and also laughed a little to myself. *He was something else.*

I resumed retrieving the pancakes and brought them to the table where my impatient friend was pounding his utensils. The whole room smelled like pancakes and I wanted to eat all twenty myself. Before I could even set the tray down Chase eagerly grabbed a few pancakes and set them on his plate. I sat down with him and put a pile on my plate too. We slathered our pancakes with butter and syrup and practically shoveled them into our mouths. Chase's exuberant scarfing was exactly what I was hoping for, and the pancakes tasted pretty good too.

"How did you sleep?" I asked Chase as I chewed the side of a slippery pancake.

Chase swallowed some food down his throat and then replied, "Surprisingly well. How 'bout you?"

I hesitated, not knowing if I should tell him about the oddly real dream. Chase was my best friend and I was grateful to him for that. Kids at school used to bully me and treat me like a loser, until Chase, a popular guy, started to defend me and then hang out with me. That was all it took to change things for me at school. I always knew I'd have the last laugh if I studied and got good grades and went to a good college because those jerks weren't going anywhere. They never put in any effort to get what they wanted. They didn't know how to apply themselves, is how Chase once put it, but I knew it would catch up with them. You can't ever fully erase your bad marks—even pencil marks only get lighter when you erase them. They never go away completely. No matter if you shred or rip it, pieces of evidence will show. Their dismal futures would be my revenge. Still, middle school was a whole lot better after Chase and I became friends. I never wanted to lose his respect, which seemed like a risk if I told him that I thought I was abducted by the T.F.G., handcuffed to a gurney on the way to meet their leader, Crofar, but which I escaped thanks to a loose screw. "Yeah, I slept okay too," I replied.

"Cool," Chase said, which was kind of a letdown. I wished that he would have noticed that I hesitated and pushed me to talk. I started to realize how important Chase was to me, now more than ever. He was always the guy that stuck up for me but now he was literally my only family. I immediately regretted not telling him about my dream, or whatever it was. *Chase never laughs or calls me a loser. Chase sticks up for me. He would take a beating if that would mean humiliation would stop. He's there for me and I am there for him.* My thoughts filled the silence at the table as Chase blissfully dug into a second helping of pancakes. I imagined people starting out like fresh pieces of paper and getting dinged up by experiences. The kids at my school tormented me and rolled my paper into a ball. But instead of crumbling me, Chase unfolded me. He unfolded my life. He taught me to laugh and how to have a good time. People started to make fun of Chase for hanging out with a "loser" but he didn't care. When I saw this, and what he did for me, I completely unfolded and my paper was no longer a ball but a rectangle with some wrinkles on it. No matter what happens, I thought, the wrinkles are permanent and the paper can never be exactly the same as it was. But Chase was the guy that smoothed it all out.

"What's that smell?" Hazel's voice broke into my thoughts and brought a smile to my face.

"I made pancakes! If you want some, you better take some before Chase polishes them off," I replied. I handed her the plate of pancakes, considerably smaller and cooler and less impressive than I wanted her to see.

"Thanks," she said as she took a seat next to me and filled her plate. Hazel spread butter and drizzled syrup on her breakfast. Chase grabbed another pancake and so did I. Spending time together with my friends felt really good and I wished I could do this forever. But there was a lot of work to do and a world to save. It was crazy that a group of teenagers was going to have to save the world. I drifted back in my mind to that dream again and what it might have meant when Hazel broke in again, "Hey, I'm sorry I was so rude to you guys yesterday at the doctor's office. I was just scared and worked up. I never thought anything as crazy as what is happening right now could ever happen. So I want to thank you guys for saving my life and putting up with my mean self."

"You weren't rude," I reassured her. "I totally understand. You were right not to trust and believe us at first. It was hard enough to tell Chase and for him to believe me and he at least knew me. This is definitely an unbelievable situation."

Hazel looked at me with tears in her eyes and then she pulled me into a hug. "Thank you," she whispered in my ear.

"Uh, hello," Chase chimed in. "I'm the one you insulted if I remember correctly."

"Oh, sorry," Hazel said as she let go of the hug and also thanked Chase. I didn't know what I was feeling but I couldn't think. My mind couldn't figure out what to do with my body. My body was still leaning forward from the hug. *What is going on with me? I've never felt this strange in my life.* "Uh, John?" Hazel laughed as she gently touched my shoulders to move my body back.

"Caught me daydreaming," I lied to her. She laughed and kept eating while I couldn't figure out how to pick up a fork. Chase and Hazel finished eating and put their plates in the sink while I sat and stared at the wall in front of me like a frozen Captain America. I still didn't know what I was feeling but I did know I liked it.

95

CHAPTER 11

All of the dishes were spotless due to my obsessive compulsiveness when it comes to cleaning, something I inherited from my mom. The plates and silverware were in the sink air drying and I was already making a plan for the rest of the day. We were good on food supplies but badly needed weapons and a laptop. I began thinking this through as I rested on my bed digesting my breakfast.

I knew we would have no problem finding an electronics store but a store that sold weapons to teenagers might be harder to come by. We should at least be able to get knives, but guns were definitely desirable under the circumstances. As I was thinking about the need to purchase weapons, I had the fleeting thought of how odd this whole situation was and about what I would be doing or feeling at that moment if my parents hadn't discovered the truth behind the T.F.G. which ultimately cost them their lives and put Chase, Hazel, and me on the run.

If all of this hadn't happened, I would have been at school looking forward to lunch with all my friends. Later I would be hanging out with Chase, playing video games to my heart's content, eating junk food, and catching up on each other's day instead of sitting on a foreign bed inside a foreign house being rented by three teens who don't have a clue what to do. Instead I was trying to figure everything out, including my dream, and had nothing going for me other than living through this nightmare with my best friend and new friend. I decided that the most important thing was that we were alive, at least for the time being.

It then dawned on me that I shouldn't be complaining about missing the good life, filled with video games and junk food, when I was really so lucky to be alive, to have a place to sleep, and food to eat. I was so lucky to have Chase and our new friend, Hazel, whom I could really trust and talk to. We would survive together, I thought, by sharing everything. We have enough money to buy the supplies we need to keep us walking on this planet. I knew I was so lucky to have them. *So then, why did I not share my pain from the dream with them? Why am I not sharing how*

hopeless I feel this mission is with them?

My room blurred as my eyes welled up with tears. One day in hiding and I was already feeling like giving up. There was nothing I could do that would take the sorrow away but I did somehow *know* that we would live to see better days. I put all this confusion to the side and tried to clearly think about the day ahead.

It was a cool 72 degrees according to my thermometer clock. Wind was breezing all through the veins of the city that made its way past the sealed glass windows of our house. Today was a perfect day to go shopping. I took out a map of the city I had found in the front of an old phone book tucked into one of the kitchen cabinets. It displayed roads, parks, and stores galore all over town.

The city of Amber looked like a big grape on the thin paper map. I looked at the map studying the street names and different places to discover. Chester Montiago Road intersected Jeff Heard Blvd. about a half mile from our house. These were main artery streets with lots of commercial options. Most of the streets were named after some hero who lived in the city but I didn't recognize a single one of them. Everything felt foreign to me.

I found the real estate store and the restaurant we had gone to the day before on the map. They looked like little ants surrounded by many stores in a circular cage on the map. Then I found the house I was in at the northern top of the circular city. It was hard to see but it was visible. I searched for an electronics store close to our house. There was one in the heart of the city, called A-Mobile. The title seemed familiar to me but I couldn't quite place it. I searched the bag I had taken with me and found a red pen with which I made a perfect circle around the store.

I studied the map more in hopes of finding an armory store. The stores were labeled so small it took me awhile to spot one on the East side. It was called Amber Arms. I circled it with red ink too. I studied the map once more before folding it neatly and putting it into my pocket. I could hear Chase moving around in his bedroom across the hall. I could also hear Hazel in hers, humming some song. There was something special about Hazel. Out of all the kids we could have taken with us on this journey, I was glad it was Hazel. She was resourceful and brave. She was strong, but also kind and sweet. She always knew the right time to say something and the right place to say it. It was nice knowing a girl with different strategies was on our team but I realized what I liked about Hazel was her attitude. She was up for anything.

I stepped outside of my new room and yelled, "Guys, meet me in the kitchen!" I went over to the kitchen table and took the map out of my pocket. I pushed it against the table to smoothen it out. I heard their doors open about the same time. Then I heard exaggerated grunts from Chase. I stood at the table with my hands on the map and waited. When I looked up, Hazel and Chase were standing on the other side of the table, looking rather annoyed about this summons. "Alright guys I have a plan for what we need to do today," I said as I waved them over to the map laid out in front of me. "This is a map of Amber City. I circled two stores that we need to stop by today. One of them is an electronics store and the other is a weapon store."

"Cool. Who's going to get the stuff?" Chase asked casually.

"Seriously?" Hazel said, exaggerating her surprise.

Chase tilted his head, meeting Hazel's sarcasm with his own. "We are currently living in a city with people and *we* are the only people on the T.F.G.'s most wanted list."

"All of us are going," I said authoritatively. "There is a "u" in "us" so that means *you*, too, Chase."

Chase dropped his head in realization that he couldn't stay home and sleep the whole day away.

"Guys, we need to work together," I said. I saw the disappointed look on Hazel's face too, as if she was also planning to stay home today. "Any suggestions or questions about the plan? Am I forgetting anything?"

"Should we get cheap flip phones for each of us in case of an emergency?" Hazel asked.

I wasn't in favor of this idea because it seemed like phones could be used to track us. "Well," I said, "since we are staying together and working as a team, phones won't be necessary." I looked at Chase to let him know that if he had anything to say he should say it, but he didn't say anything. "Okay. Well. Let's go then," I stammered as we headed to our front door.

Hazel looked excited now but Chase just looked sad and tired. I wondered what was up with him but this wasn't the time to ask.

As a group we left our safe space and followed the back route I had mapped out that led to the electronics store. We constantly looked for street signs and roads and then back at the map which I held in front of me. The side streets on our route were quiet and the breeze created a nice environment for our walk. After about a half hour we turned onto a busy street and saw an electronics store with "A-Mobile" in bright lights posted on the building. The outside of the building was like an amusement park with lights all around advertising phones and cellular services.

We pulled the door open as a chime rang throughout the store. In front of us were displays full of phones and different types of technology. To our right we saw a woman staring at us with that weird smile I have seen millions of times. I smiled back and looked around the store. Chase and Hazel went in opposite directions looking for laptops. I stayed put and scanned the area around me for valuable equipment. I was in the section where you could find cool attachments for computers and phones. There were chargers of different colors and keyboards and cases. I found an awesome phone case that was transparent but I didn't need it since we weren't getting phones at all.

Chase and Hazel were in the back of the store so I went to where they were. They were checking out a nice black laptop that wasn't too expensive but had the required technology in it. They noticed my presence so they turned around.

"I see you found a laptop," I said.

"Yup, and it's perfect for what we need to do," Hazel said with a smile.

"That's great," I replied, looking at her hands on the laptop's shiny skin. "I couldn't find anything useful in the front of the store, only chargers and cases."

"That's fine. We don't need anything besides this laptop so you're good," Chase said.

"Feels good to be up and moving, doesn't it?" I asked them.

"Yeah, I guess you're right. I've been happier since we left. It's good to get our minds off of what happened yesterday," Chase replied.

"Yesterday? It feels like ages since I sat in the medical building," remarked Hazel.

"You're right. It has felt like we've been here a lot longer than we have," I agreed.

Chase bent down and pulled a box from underneath a display stand. He handed the black box with a photo of the laptop on the front of it to me. It was pretty light so I didn't mind carrying it. "Ready to go?" I asked, to which they both nodded.

We made our way up to the cashier and I lifted the laptop so she could scan it. She typed some things on the computer in front of her that I couldn't see. The whole time that she typed, she showed no expression at all. I didn't think she was even looking at the screen while inputting the information although she was staring at us. Man, I was so happy that I didn't turn into her. I gave her enough money to pay for the laptop and she handed me back the change. From under the desk, she pulled out a bag and put the laptop and receipt in it. Once the laptop was in the bag, she handed it to me and said, "Thank you for coming. Please come back soon." She said this with the usual creepy smile that remained on her face the whole time she watched us as we walked towards the exit. Once we left the store, the three of us burst out laughing. It was such a relief to get out of there, and to laugh.

After a few minutes of jokes about robots selling computers, we pulled ourselves together and started walking towards the weapon store. We had to cross many streets but it was an easy walk because barely anyone was out on the roads, either driving or walking. On the way, I noticed bricks turned into smooth concrete on the sidewalks. There was less and less civilization as we made our way to the East side. It made sense that a weapon store was in a low populated area. I wondered what other types of stores would be out here, where people weren't walking outside, or walking their dogs, or biking, or driving. Their absence was really noticeable. I thought this would be a good place for the T.F.G. to be headquartered.

We reached our destination and I began having bad feelings about the type of people who could be controlled here. I was hoping that the T.F.G. wasn't looking for us through hidden cameras, but that seemed like a real possibility. The store was windowless and had a dull "Amber Arms" painted in silver on the dark grey wall. In this city it was obvious which stores were safer than others.

"This is it," I said with a shaky voice.

"Are you sure there aren't any other places we could go to?" Chase asked in a hopeful voice as he stared at the run-down building.

"Nope. This is the only one," I told Chase in an apologetic tone.

Chase and I looked back down at the map anyway and scoured it for another place as Hazel came up from behind us and said, "You are such a wimp!"

"Well you know what?" Chase asked bouncing up and down thinking about comebacks.

"What?" Hazel asked with an eyebrow raised. She didn't think he could come up with something and from past experience I knew she was right.

"You are a wimp, too." Chase then dropped an invisible mic and then went to give me a high-five, as if this alone would make his comeback respectable. I, of course, did not give him a high-five. He was entertaining but this was not what we needed right now. Chase was about as useful as a screen door on a submarine. I left him empty handed which turned his grin into blankness and then a frown. He knew he should just stay quiet.

"Does he always act stupid like this?" Hazel asked, as if she were really worried.

"I'm afraid so," I answered, trying to match her pretense of doom.

Just then the door flung open and I smelled dust and felt it on my skin. The dust particles were everywhere causing me to cough. I covered my mouth but couldn't stop coughing. "You ok?" I heard someone say. I looked around and then noticed the guy who spoke behind the counter. He was the biggest, meanest looking cashier I had ever seen. He was wearing a black long sleeve shirt that was torn in some places along with grey jeans. His look matched the store's look perfectly.

"It only gets creepier," Hazel whispered to me.

The guy was staring at us intently, and I was staring at him too but out of fear. I quickly responded to his question, "I'm just a little sick." He then turned his gaze from me to his desk. I took this gesture as a sign that we could continue on with our shopping.

"That was kind of weird," Hazel whispered to me curiously.

"Yeah, I don't think I trust him," I said.

"Why not?" Hazel asked. "He hasn't done anything to harm us. Do you think he will? I mean, harm us?"

"I'm a little scared of him," Chase murmured in a mouse-like voice.

"You're scared of everything," I said, stepping in front of him and turning to Hazel. I knew I was being rude to my best friend but I needed him to be tougher. "He just doesn't look like the rest of the people here," I said to Hazel as I scanned the room for weapons that would be useful.

"Well, someone is racist," Hazel quickly snapped.

"I don't mean it like that Hazel," I said angrily. "I mean that I don't think he's being controlled by the T.F.G." Just as I said this I heard someone come up behind me. I spun around and a stocky man with a heavily tattooed neck was smiling at me.

"Nice to see you, John," the man said. "We've been waiting for you." He apparently knew me, but I had no idea how.

"What is going on?!" I demanded, now very worried that something was not right.

"Why don't you ask my friend, Crofar?" the man said as he moved out of the way for someone. A lanky man then appeared in front of us with a mischievous smile on his face. He had short hair and a short graze of facial hair from his chin to his head. He wore a commander's uniform and he had a silver chain around his neck.

I had definitely heard this name, Crofar, before. I had heard it from one of the soldiers in my dream the night before. I didn't know any details about this Crofar but I knew he was a bad man. And here he was. Crofar lifted his head higher and said, "I see you recognize me, John. Well guess what? I recognize you too."

"What is he talking about?" Hazel asked. "Obviously this guy knows you. What are you not telling us?"

"I don't know him," I said, as I tried to figure out what was going on myself. In my dream, I was supposed to meet Crofar, but I didn't remember meeting him. Then Crofar started laughing.

"I guess you and I are the only ones that *know*, John. You know what I mean?" he said, not quite looking at me. I desperately tried to understand what was happening, like kids do when they first learn division. I started to sweat.

"John, what is he talking about?!" Hazel said, looking pissed. Or disappointed. Or both. Chase's expression was more like sheer bewilderment. He looked at me and then turned to face Crofar. The little tattooed man stood alongside Crofar, and they were both laughing at us. But there was something different about these two guys. One guy had lines etched into his cheeks and forehead. His eyebrows were raised in laughter. His little body was bouncing up and down when he laughed, but he also looked a little scared. He was vulnerable. Maybe even weak. But Crofar had less character, just laughing as if he were invincible. Something was off but I couldn't tell what it was.

"Your team is pathetic," Crofar started, "but mine is huge and well-armed. We outnumber you hundreds to three. I would recommend giving up your childish hopes of destroying an empire. You will lose, John, just like your parents lost, and I don't want you to have to see your friends die too."

He knew exactly what to say to make me grit my teeth and clench my fists. "You want to see who has the odds?" I yelled, lunging a step toward Crofar, ready to fight. Chase and Hazel in unison grabbed me on each side, and Crofar just kept laughing.

"I want them alive. Take them," Crofar casually told his little henchman, who obediently pounded the floor with his boots and reached for his knife. *This is ridiculous!* I thought. *How is this one guy going to take all three of us??*

"This will be easy," the man said as he grinned like a mad fool and held his knife out to threaten us.

"You're kidding, right?!" I yelled. "We aren't afraid of you and your silly blade. There are three of us, dumbass!"

"Tell that to the soldiers behind you," he quipped. Out of nowhere I got tackled from behind. I hit the floor before I could get my hands under me. Then someone hurled himself onto my back and brutally forced my hands together behind me and clasped them.

111

"We're taking you in," I heard a deep voice say from behind me.

"I don't think so," someone else said. I thought I was hearing things because the voice was not Chase's or Hazel's. All of a sudden the man behind me dropped my hands, freeing me. I had no idea what was happening but I could hear grunts and slams happening all over the store. I stood up to see Chase and Hazel pushing themselves back up on opposite sides of the aisle. In the center of the aisle was a tall buff man pointing a gun at Crofar with four soldiers on the floor in front of him. One of them was the tattooed guy.

It didn't take me long to realize that the man who saved us was the shifty-looking cashier we encountered earlier. I had pegged him as mean, rude, and definitely petrifying. "Put your hands behind your cocky little head or I will shoot a bullet straight through it," the cashier said as he motioned the gun at Crofar.

"Aw, that's cute," Crofar returned. "But today I am only following my rules."

"Oh really?" the cashier hissed. "You know what? I've been hunting you down my whole life so I think I'm going to shoot you anyway."

Crofar kept chuckling like a maniac while the cashier pulled the trigger and a death-searching bullet pierced the air.

Time crawled through that moment and I watched the bullet go straight through Crofar but never puncture him. I was left in shock—the kind of shock where you feel the need to close your mouth because your jaw is left hanging open. *How is this possible?* Then I saw Crofar's body—or rather, his image—shift to one side and then snap back to before. "Adios!" Crofar said, still laughing, and he immediately disappeared like he had never been there. Well, he never was there. My attention was then focused on a small circular object on the floor where Crofar stood seconds ago. The object was a hologram.

We all stood there fixated on the spot where our destiny once stood, or so we thought. One of the soldiers broke the silence with an effort to get up. The cashier, still staring at the empty space on the floor, forcefully pushed the soldier's head down with his foot. The soldier went limp with a crack. None of us spoke. The only sound that could be heard was the wind howling through the cracks between the doors. I imagined it blowing through every nook and cranny in this little city. All of us stood there still and stiff, as if we were the dead soldiers.

"Who was that?!" Chase asked turning towards me. I opened my mouth to answer but I was interrupted by the buff cashier. "That was Crofar, or the image of him. He is the leader of the T.F.G., which stands for Tracker for Globe. You kids haven't got your shot yet, right?" he asked.

"No. Have you gotten *your* shots yet?" I asked suspiciously.

He looked me up and down and a half-smile came across his face. I wasn't sure what he was smiling about and I was tired of all the irritating posturing. I grabbed a small dagger from the shelf next to me and held it tightly in front of me.

"Whoa! Whoa! Whoa! You don't need to worry about me," the cashier claimed. "I'm on your side."

"Then why were you giving us a death glare when we came in?" Hazel asked, raising her voice as she walked over to join me. Chase and Hazel stood behind me, bolstering our chances if this little exchange were to become a fight.

He completely ignored Hazel. "Dude, if you try to take me with that knife, the rest of my group will kill you," the cashier said in a confident voice. "Use your head," he finished.

"What group?" I asked as I raised my dagger a little higher to show him that I wasn't backing down.

"We call ourselves the Renegades," he replied. "Long story short, we have the opposite goals of the T.F.G. Like you, we want to end them and their stupid plan to control everyone's minds. Our base is held in an alleyway some ways from here. There are about thirty of us who did not get our shots and are constantly planning to destroy the T.F.G."

An alleyway not too far from here? I thought, zeroing in on this one sliver of his explanation. Goosebumps crawled up the back of my spine as I wondered if this was the alleyway I had walked through almost every day coming home from Chase's.

"If you have a base and are constantly working on plans, why are you here in Amber City?" Chase asked, surprising me that he had come up with such a brilliant question.

"We came here because we heard about the mayhem at the doctor's office and of course we were interested in it. We got there toward the end and saw you guys running towards Amber. We knew you'd need weapons so we planted ourselves here and waited. Good plan, I'd say."

"What do you want with us?" I asked, lowering my dagger.

"We want to recruit you," he said. "We think you guys will be a great addition to our efforts to stop the T.F.G., and I have a feeling you are going to need us too."

"Give us a second please," I said to him. I turned around and pulled my friends farther away from the cashier. "Do you trust him?" I asked both of them.

"I don't know," Hazel spoke first. "If you put all of this together it kind of makes sense, but I don't think we should commit our lives to them just yet."

Chase paused and took a deep breath. He looked like a kid on Halloween whose mother just told him he was allergic to sugar. "Whatever she says."

With that we turned around and faced the cashier. "I think we are going to need some time to decide," I told him.

"Fine," he responded, "but soon you will realize that you should have come with us earlier." He reached down into his pocket and pulled out a small rectangular device with buttons on it. It was clearly not a regular cell phone. He handed it to me and spoke slowly, "When you decide, you can reach me with this. Press the green button to call and the red to decline or cancel anything."

I took the device from his hands and wrapped my fingers around it. Just like he described, there was a small green square on the left of it and a red one on the right. Both buttons were covered so they wouldn't be accidentally pressed. I wondered why they didn't just use phones.

"I forgot to mention, my name is Maximus and I'm the leader of the Renegades. Decide soon if you're going to work with us," he added, "obviously the T.F.G. is looking for you too. What they really want is to give you that shot so they can control you like everyone else. So until you decide that you want to work with

CHAPTER 12

When we got home we were all acting weird. I noticed how different my thoughts were compared to when we had left just a few short hours before. Chase and Hazel were both quiet, obviously trying to process what just happened. This worried me. They could be thinking about what Crofar was saying about recognizing me. If Crofar recognized me, it must mean he's seen me somewhere in the past. But where? In my dream they were taking me to meet him but it didn't happen in real life. Or did it? That's what was bothering me—I couldn't be sure if my dreams were really dreams, or visions, or what. As far as I knew I was the only one who knew about this little problem—or power—of mine, and I wanted to keep it that way.

Hazel broke my train of thought, trying not to sound like a broken record, "Time to fess up, John. What was holo-man talking about when he said he knew you?"

"I have been thinking about that also," I admitted. "I've never seen that man in my life!" That may have been true. I was so confused. "He did sound like he knew a lot more about us than we did about him. Creepy dude."

"Creepy dude is correct," Chase said, being his usual jokester self. "And it's so weird that he knew who John was. I mean, I'm more famous than this hunka junka."

I was kind of annoyed again. Chase never seems to get how serious our situation is—*these people want to control us*. "Oh, come on!" I said, exaggerating my frustration. "This is not a popularity contest."

"That's it! I've got it!" Chase exclaimed.

Hazel and I looked at each other and then back to Chase. We both thought he was about to say something stupid when Chase jumped up with excitement and said, "Popularity is key!" Chase held up both of his hands with his pointer fingers sticking up. I knew the wheels in his head were turning because he started blurting out a plan from nowhere. "Crofar is the leader of the T.F.G., right? That means he's popular, at least with the T.F.G. They have to communicate. If they communicate, there has to be a signal, a trail. We can use our new laptop to find Crofar. If we find him, we can capture him. Well, maybe. That might be tricky since he seems to know a thing or two about not being where you think he is. Anyway, I still think we can find him. Maybe find his base. That's step one. You two can worry about what we do when we find him. That's above my pay grade."

Chase was so excited about his lightbulb moment that he shoved me to the side to get to the bag of electronics. He immediately took out the laptop and ran to the table in front of us. I knew that if he got a glimpse of an idea we should let him work on it because Chase could be like a little Einstein at times. I looked back at Hazel to see what she thought about it. Her face was glowing with excitement also. She looked at me and mouthed, "He's *smart*?!" I could tell that Hazel had never seen this side of Chase. But I had. It reminded me of all the times I would come to his house to play video games—the moment when he would find a clue something would light up in him and he would win the game.

I felt bad for being so annoyed with Chase. He is going to come through after all, I thought. I looked to the stove in the kitchen and the clock said it was 6:00 p.m. "I'm hungry," I suddenly realized. "Do you want to eat out or in?"

Without even looking up from the laptop Chase said, "Out."

Hazel watched Chase work and shook her head in disbelief. "I say, in," she said to me. "I don't want to risk leaving this house again until tomorrow."

I declared my agreement with Hazel. Eating in was safer and Chase could keep working on the laptop. The sooner he found Crofar, the better. But I wasn't in the mood to make any food. My friends both seemed kind of helpless when it came to cooking. I could feel them both staring at me like I was wearing a chef's hat or something. "What?" I responded to their stares. "Help yourself to dinner. It's all you can eat. Or eat whatever you can find. It's *self*-serve!" I brushed past them and opened the fridge. I saw what I was looking for and pulled out the big pie I bought at the grocery store. I cut a slice from it to take to my room. I was momentarily stopped by Chase who must have been paying attention without letting on. "Awesome idea, John. Can you get me a slice? Please?"

"Didn't you hear what I told Hazel?" I yelled. "What? Am I your nanny now?"

Chase finally looked up. "Hey, I'm working on finding our enemy and your arch-nemesis. So cut me some slack. A friend would get me some food."

I'm not sure why—maybe because he was right—but I dug in. "If you were smart like this all the time I *would* get you a slice. But that is not the case. So feed yourself!"

I walked toward my room with my slice of pie and heard Hazel give Chase a similar brush-off. "Oh get roasted!" I heard her say, and then some chairs scraping the floor. I assumed that Chase had finally gotten up to get his own pie. I closed the door of my room and set my pie down on the nightstand. Then I hopped on the bed letting my legs dangle over the side and stared at the grey wall in front of me.

I forced myself to remain in a focused state of mind and considered the plan Chase was pursuing. Finding Crofar was going to be harder than Chase thinks. Crofar isn't the mayor or president. It's not like he has appointments or speeches that he gives in public. We might have to lure him out into the public. But how? And even if we find him, how will we capture him and take him back as a prisoner? We would need some type of tranquilizer to knock him out. Or maybe we could just use our weapons to force him to follow us. That might work better but Crofar has a huge society of people who can also successfully kill. If we find him out in the open there is no doubt that he will be surrounded by soldiers or security guards. If we wanted to get through to him we would have to get through his men who are loaded with guns and other lethal equipment. A trio of teenagers isn't going to beat down many grown men. We would need a bigger team. We would need the Renegades' help but I still had my suspicions about them. How do we know if we can trust them?

I threw my head in my hands. This was crazy! I had to chase before I could fight, I had to choose between teams, and I had to find out if I actually had oracle super-powers. The earth was turning too fast. I released my head from my hands and broke my gaze from the wall. I reached over to grab the slice of pie I took. It was half eaten. I took the last half in my hand and finished it. I barely even tasted it because I was so weary from the shopping, fighting, and thinking. My body needed sleep and I was looking forward to the night. Maybe I would have another vision and I would know what to do.

I stood up from my bed and brought the pie plate to the kitchen. Chase was sitting in the same spot, the light from the laptop flickering on his face. I didn't see Hazel anywhere. "Hey, I'm sorry about before. I'm just stressed working on the plan. Is Hazel asleep?"

"Yeah," Chase said and we exchanged good-nights. I returned to my pitch-black room with my arms stretched out, feeling for objects that might be in the way of my bed. When I found my bed I plopped right on it. This bed in this little rental home was so comfortable. I tried to think more about our plan to find Crofar but I couldn't. My mind went to rest.

CHAPTER 13

I expected there to be nothing wedged between sleep and reality but there was something there. It was a vision. I didn't realize I was in it at first but then I felt familiar objects around me. I was back on the little platform under the metal bed. I then heard feet shuffling away from me. I poked my head to the side to see who it was. I could only see shoes and legs but I was pretty sure they belonged to Hazel and Chase. "Where the hell is he?!"

I recognized this voice. "Hazel?" I said out loud.

Chase and Hazel turned around. I felt relief even though I had no idea what was going on. It was the same vision as before, but later. It was like waking up and living through another day, just put the vision on hold, until I could fall asleep again. They looked around in frustration trying to find me. I rolled out of my hiding spot so that they could see me. "John, you look terrible! Let me help you up," Hazel said, running toward me. She was carrying a gun and I could see the gold and black insignia of Amber Arms on the side of it. With her other arm she reached out to me. I grabbed on and she pulled me to my feet with such strength that I almost fell over the other way.

"Alright let's get out of here and fast before they take you captive again," Hazel said.

"Again?" I asked, feeling confused. In my previous vision, I was the only one who was captive. At least that's what I had thought. How did they capture us in the first place? That's what I wanted to be having a vision of. Then maybe I could prevent that and avoid all of this.

Hazel looked at me wearing her own confusion. "Did they mess with your brain, John?"

"No," I told her, wondering if they had. I wasn't sure how I would know.

"Then stop acting like Chase," she joked as I struggled to put the pieces together. We must have tried something to stop the T.F.G. and it didn't work. Maybe we shouldn't be looking for Crofar. Chase was standing next to me and I could feel him staring at me. I turned to face him and his expression caught me off guard.

"Dude. You look like a ghost. Is everything okay?" I asked him. His expression changed. He looked at me like I was the dumbest person on the planet, which is obviously not true because almost the whole planet is brainwashed.

"Is everything okay?," he yelled, parroting my question.

"You tell me. Do you think I should be okay after my amazingly brilliant plan fails so badly that we are all taken captive? Do you think I should be okay that we still have to find our way out of this terrifying nightmare? Do you think I should be okay with you being beaten up by these T.F.G. zombies?"

I was blown away by Chase's anger. I had never heard him yell like this except when we fought on the way to Amber. This time though it seemed like he was mad at himself—like it was his fault we were here. Then my mind turned to what he said. *Was I beaten up?* I started to remember the last vision and as I brought my hand to my face the pain roared to life. At the same time, alarms everywhere started blinking on and off while making insanely loud noises. The T.F.G. must have realized that we had all escaped our kept places and were on the move. Hazel motioned and Chase and I followed her down that same long hallway that I came through in my last vision. I could no longer hear our footsteps as we went through a couple of doors. The hallways we went through changed from pitch black to bright white and back. It was hard not to lose my balance. There were no guards to stop us so we continued onward. I didn't know how Hazel and Chase knew how to get out of here but I stayed behind them at a jogging pace. Hazel stopped suddenly and I almost slid into her. "Stay here!" Hazel ordered.

"What?! I am not going to stay here like a sitting duck. We need to move," Chase yelled to Hazel over the loud alarms. Hazel ignored him and sprinted ahead to the end of the path. To the right of her was a corner which she peeked around. Hazel immediately pulled back. Whatever she saw was not good. I had no idea what she was doing, what I was doing, or what Chase was doing. Questions came to my mind as I stayed back with Chase; questions about how they knew where they were going, whether this was real or a vision of the future. I wondered if I could change this future if it doesn't go well.

I decided to take a chance and ask Chase how they knew where they were going. Just as I opened my mouth to ask the question Chase started talking. "Hey, I'm sorry if I hurt you with what I said earlier. I wasn't thinking and I was so scared that I took it out on you. The T.F.G. might have cleared some of your memory but I don't know. I'm sorry." I stood there not knowing what to feel. Why did he think I had lost my memory? I stopped short of asking him for more information. There wasn't time. "Thanks," I said. "I am also sorry."

Hazel gave us the all clear, and Chase and I looked at each other curiously. *Where is everybody?* We followed her down to the end of this hallway and then we took a right. As soon as we turned we saw four soldiers lying on the floor in puddles of blood. They were all wearing the same familiar uniform, and guns were strewn about the floor. Chase looked at me as we jogged through them and mouthed, "Holy crap. Did Hazel seriously just kill four men?" I was shocked too. I knew that they were the enemy but she just killed them in the time it took Chase to apologize to me.

We kept jogging behind Hazel as she led us down more jagged turns. If this was the T.F.G.'s base then it was surely huge.

Hazel seemed to know where she was going, but I didn't know how. I was super-tired from all the running and all the punches that had been thrown at me. And yet somehow I knew that this was a vision and that I was really sleeping in my bed. But I had no control of it. The lights on the ceiling flickered on and off continuously. The sirens were blaring. The lights and sounds mixed together and I was feeling like I was going to be sick. I closed my eyes and covered my ears and sank to the floor in a huddle. The pain was more than I could handle.

The sirens were soon overpowered by a voice. "Sorry John, but we have to move or we will get caught again!" Chase yelled over the sounds. He pulled me up and forward with him. I shuddered and stumbled at first but soon regained some of my strength.

"However we're going to get out of here, let's make it fast!" I said, pretending that I was good to go.

"Let's go!" Hazel yelled, and we were off running again through the maze of hallways. My pain helped me focus the questions in my mind. Even though lights were flashing in my face and sirens were blaring in my ears, questions arose to the top of the senses chain. The main question was about how I might control my visions but I also had questions like what day it was and whether I should tell Hazel and Chase that I have these visions.

Two soldiers jumped in front of us right before we turned the corner. I barely saw them because Hazel easily dropped them using a gun she had in a holster. I had no idea that she could even shoot a gun but soldiers rarely had a chance to pull the trigger before Hazel did. Chase seemed unsurprised, like he had seen this before, but I was shocked. Chase could tell what I was thinking because he said, "Wow, they totally cleared your memory."

"I thought you apologized for saying that!" I yelled over the noises.

"Oh yeah, my bad." Chase had a knife in one hand and something else in the other. It looked like a map. Hazel interrupted my train of thought.

"There's about a dozen soldiers turning the corner ahead."

Chase immediately stopped moving and stared in front of us. I followed his stare and saw that Hazel was right. There were at least twelve T.F.G. soldiers standing in formation many feet in front of us. Hazel handed me a knife and said, "This is going to be a hell of a fight."

"A knife?!" I remarked. "They all have guns!"

"Is Chase complaining?" Hazel asked, turning back to face the soldiers because she knew she had won the argument. I looked at the knife she gave me and saw the Amber Arms logo on the side of it. This was definitely a vision of the future. The knife was matte black with one very sharp edge. The handle was embroidered in different shapes overlapping one another. Hazel took her left hand and reached into what looked like another holster. I couldn't make it out because she was wearing a grey jacket with designer holes in it.

The soldiers just stood there looking at us, waiting for us to make a move. No one talked but the background noise got louder and louder, wanting to be the main sound. One of the soldiers lifted a rifle and Hazel began shooting at the soldiers. Chase and I found cover around a corner while Hazel kept firing at them. I could see that she hit two guys very quickly but there were too many. The other soldiers started shooting and Hazel sprinted back towards us.

Then I saw something terrible happen. As Hazel was running back a bullet grazed her shoulder. Blood came seeping through her shirt and jacket. As soon as she made it to us she put her guns down and held her shoulder, trying to ease the pain and slow the blood. I let Chase tend to her while I picked up the pistols and fired one at a time around the corner. I was shooting blindly because they were firing constantly. I watched bullets go through the wall in front of me as I reloaded the guns.

Hazel needed bandages to wrap around her arm and Chase was tearing up his shirt to give her some aid. While I was reloading, the sirens stopped. Now all I could hear were the booms coming from the muzzles of guns. The lights were still pulsing and when they were off the hall was lit up from the shots being fired. I finished reloading with the last mag of ammo Hazel gave me. I turned around the corner to shoot again but I was sidetracked by the whole place shaking. A few lights fell down from the ceiling and crashed, and the wall on our right was shaking so violently that I thought it was going to tumble over and

134

smash all of us. But instead of falling over, the wall was torn apart by something moving. At least twenty people wearing helmets and holding guns jumped through the wall. That's way more than we can take, I thought.

I turned to Hazel and Chase and they looked stunned. This was it, I thought. Through the break in the wall, I could see offices full of computers, gadgets, and tracking systems. If these people came through from the offices they must work with the T.F.G. Chase already had his arms up in surrender. Hazel had one arm up surrendering but she couldn't lift her left arm because of her wound. I followed my friends' actions and put the two pistols down. I then lifted my hands but I knew something was off. When I looked closely at the men, I could see what it was. They weren't facing us, they were facing the T.F.G.

There was a sudden blast of gunfire and as quickly as lightning the men that came through the wall had eliminated all the remaining soldiers. Was this an uprising in the T.F.G. base? This was crazy! T.F.G. members against T.F.G. members was the best thing I could imagine. This would mean that Chase, Hazel, and I could sit on a beach drinking coconut milk while waiting for the T.F.G. to collapse on its own.

I was just about to tell Hazel and Chase that we were the beneficiaries of a T.F.G. uprising when the lethal rebellion turned toward us and started walking fast in our direction. I shoved my friends in the direction we came. We started sprinting faster than I thought we ever could. We could hear yells from the people behind us but we ignored them, more desperate than ever to get out of there.

Once we were a safe distance from the helmeted men we stopped to catch our breath. "Listen," I told my friends, "If they could hop through a wall then we can, right? I don't think there is any other way out."

Hazel sighed and threw the right side of her body at the wall. She bounced off the wall and slid to the floor.

"Seriously?!" Chase asked as he helped her up. "Are you ok?"

"Get me out of here and I will be." Hazel said as she strained to get up. Her bullet wound had stopped bleeding but it started again and she was in even more pain.

The yells and shouts became louder but we were sitting ducks. Hazel was injured and could barely move. I had accidentally left the two guns back at the hallway where the uprising occurred so Chase and I were stuck with knives for weapons which were going to be of no use against an army of people equipped with guns. Chase's expression was priceless as he let his body fall limp against the wall and then slide down its surface to the floor. I could see in his eyes that he was trying to decide if it was better to get shot or be slowly tortured by men in full headed helmets. He stared at his knife, turned it over in his hand, and then set it carefully on his knees. "They are not going to get me alive, without a fight. That's for sure," he said quietly.

Hazel put an arm on my shoulder to get balance. She was hurt but only needed my balance to help her get a small throwing knife out of her shoe. I was starting to expect Hazel to have hiding places for weapons and other important things. That knife was probably the last weapon she had. She brought her arm back to her side and switched the weapon from her left hand to her right hand. All of us waited there next to each other with our weak

CHAPTER 14

Morning light streamed through the window of my bedroom and woke me up. This light was so different from the light in my vision. This light eased into the world of darkness and overpowered it slowly. It welcomed people and animals into its warmth. It quietly invited people to move and resume activities. This light was like a friend gently reminding me that even though there were mysteries to solve and troubles to endure, I was not alone. I opened my eyes wide and breathed in its message. I let the light make me whole. I let the light help me think. I let the light in.

I got up from my bed feeling a little different. My body had come to its senses. This time I knew that my dream was a vision; a vision of a reality that hadn't yet come to pass. Maybe that made it changeable. I suddenly felt like I knew what my purpose was. Destroying the T.F.G. might be possible by changing the present, and I was ready to accept that responsibility.

I was ready to bear the weight of changing the present to create a better future. And this time I had the light on my side.

It used to take me one to two hours to get out of my bed, but today I was wide awake. I felt light and strong, maybe because of all the exercise and running I was doing while sleeping. Or maybe because I was sleeping and not doing all that exercise and running. I pushed off the floor using my heels and my toes. I was like a spring and so were my thoughts. The questions kept coming as I put on my clothes--the same clothes I had been wearing for days! The questions were the same ones I had in the dream: mainly, was I "dreaming" some version of a future reality that could be changed? I had to find out. But if I tried to get answers from Chase and Hazel by telling them about the visions, who knows how that might change things!

One arm got through a dirty disgusting sleeve. The other arm eventually got through too--I just had to pretend that it was a new shirt. Maybe pretending could help me figure out how to tell my friends about my visions. I imagined telling them everything, but I couldn't get a clear picture of how they would react. If they realized that I was speaking the truth, what would they do? And how would that affect the outcome? The possibilities seemed endless and the more they knew, the less control I would have. *If* I had any control at all, which was still a big *if.* Two dirty socks on and two feet prepared to be covered in shoes.

Then it occurred to me that I have two sets of friends, the Chase and Hazel of the present and the Chase and Hazel of the future. If I were to tell them, which pair of friends would I tell first? I could wait until my next vision, assuming there would be one, and tell my friends in the future first. In that case I would wake up after telling my friends but my friends would not know about my visions since I hadn't told them yet. However, if I told my now-friends now, my future-friends in the vision would already know. All of this made my mind go haywire. I stood up fully clothed and all I could think about was how bad my clothes smelled.

I hadn't found time to get new clothes. If I didn't get some new clothes soon, I'd be reminded by the stench constantly, or worse, I'd get used to it. The sunlight from my window was only getting brighter and was urging me to eat. I opened my door trying to make no sounds so that Chase and Hazel could sleep but

I was mistaken. Chase was sitting at the kitchen table with papers spread out in front of him. He never took his eyes off of the papers to look at the food he was eating but he did take his eyes off them to look at me. "Rise and shine, princess!" Chase said to me with an exhausted smile.

"You weren't up all night working on your plan, were you?" I asked even though it was obvious that he had been up all night working on his plan.

"Oh yes I was!" he replied, rather proudly.

This was distressing. If he was up all night dedicating his time to the plan that fails in the future, how was I going to stop him? He looked back down at his work and pointed his finger toward the kitchen counter and offered, "If you want cereal it's on the counter."

I walked over to the counter to make myself breakfast. As I poured the cereal I asked him, "So what did you find?"

He kept at the papers and spoke through his cereal, "I found out that there is a source of radiation in this city that does not correspond to anything. *Anything!*" he said to emphasize some obscure point.

"And?" I inquired.

"Come here and I will show you what I mean." he said with a little exasperation, like I was a complete idiot. I finished making my breakfast and took my bowl and spoon and sat next to Chase. I was excited to see what he came up with. He picked up one of the many pieces of papers and showed it to me. It was a hand drawn image of the layout of a building. "This is what I found."

I immediately knew what it was a picture of but I didn't want to let on that I already knew. "What is it a picture of?" I asked.

"I think it's their base." Chase said excitedly. He had this same look whenever he solved a really hard math problem, or figured out how to get to the next level of a video game. "I was searching for radiation given off by people and of course I saw many predictable signatures but then I saw a blur of radiation all in one spot. I thought that if everyone was sleeping why would there be people clustered in the middle of the streets?" Chase explained.

Chase knows how to search for radiation signatures? "Yeah, that's weird. Maybe there are objects in the area giving off the same amount of radiation as humans?" I suggested trying to sound smart even as I knew that Chase had indeed somehow found their base. My visions convinced me that there was a base but I didn't know where it was.

"That's what I was thinking," Chase said, "but then I tracked the movement of discrete patterns of radiation and noticed that they were all moving. So I started sketching their movements. I went through many drafts but then I got the final one which is the one I am holding!"

Discrete patterns of radiation? Who is this guy? "So you're basically telling me that you tracked the movements of ghosts?" I asked him, maintaining an air of disbelief about what he was saying.

"No, John, they are *underground!* I sketched passageways based on their movements. The T.F.G. has an underground base!"

I grabbed the piece of paper out of his hand and analyzed it. This all made sense to me now. In my dream we were underground and Chase and Hazel knew where they were going

144

because of this map that Chase made of the base. I searched the map for clues about where I was on that metal bed and then the route we took to try to get out. In my vision, our whole journey through the base was literally mapped out in the sketch. I saw that we were heading towards the bottom of the map in my vision. That must be the exit, I thought.

But then my mind started tripping on another puzzle. If my visions were of the future, then I should have known where we were going too because I am looking at this map now. Chase kept telling me in the vision that the T.F.G. must have messed with my memory. When did they mess with my memory? If I could have a vision of the future but then have my memory partially erased, what good was the vision anyway?

"Can you get me a map of Amber?" Chase asked without looking up at me. This meant that Chase realized or found something important. I quickly got out of my seat and grabbed the map of Amber City that I had found in the old phone book. I handed him the map and Chase nodded his head while placing a spoonful of cereal in his mouth. "We need to figure out where the entrances and exits are in the base," he said, spraying a little milk on the map.

I stood up and cleared some space on the table. I set the drawing and the map next to each other and immediately noticed a similarity. So I put the drawing of the base on top of the map and lifted them to the light from the bulb on the ceiling. I could see the faint outlines of the drawing over the circular area of Amber city. As I shifted the placement of the drawing I locked onto an almost exact match between what Chase had drawn and a large portion of the city. I was left breathless. We were living right over our enemy's base.

"Look at this!" I said to Chase. I passed the papers to him and he held it directly to the light like I did. I reached for my spoon and took a bite of my cereal, which was getting soggy. Many of the little Os were disintegrating into the pool of milk.

"You've got to be kidding me!" Chase said, obviously seeing what I wanted him to see. "We're on a, we're on a..." Chase continued, but was interrupted by Hazel standing behind us.

"We're on a what?" Hazel asked, moving in to see what we were looking at. She looked groggy from sleep. Chase handed her the overlay of papers and brought her hand up so she could see it against the light. After a few seconds she sighed, "I don't even know what I'm looking at. How about a hint?"

"The paper on the top is an image Chase drew of the T.F.G.'s base, which is a long story, and the map on the bottom is Amber City. Notice this point here?" I said, pointing to a spot on the map, "*That* is where we live."

Hazel then brought the papers back up to the light and scanned the image. She still seemed a little out of it. "Am I supposed to be happy, angry, or surprised?"

"Are you kidding me?" Chase screamed. "We are living on top of the T.F.G.'s base!"

"It could be a good thing," I interjected. "Since the T.F.G. is underneath us we won't need to search for them and they are really close. A little bit too close but..." I said, not sure how to make that seem okay.

That didn't sit well with Chase. "Dude, what if we are sleeping or eating breakfast and then out of nowhere a squad of

147

T.F.G. comes in and takes us? Or kills us? I say we take this information and attack them first. We will have the element of surprise on our side, but only if we do this soon."

"Whoa. They know we are in the city but they don't know where our house is!" Hazel exclaimed, trying to comfort Chase, or herself.

"Yet," I said, thinking about my visions of the future. "Listen, if we follow through with Chase's idea and attack the T.F.G. base, we will fail."

"And how could you possibly know that?" Chase said angrily.

"I just do. You have to trust me!" I pleaded. I was not ready to tell them about my visions but I didn't know how else to keep us out of that base. Maybe I would stall them, I thought, but Chase was already too mad to switch gears.

"I am not letting all of my hours of work go unused and wasted. I don't see you offering a better plan and I'm not going to just sit here and wait for them to come get me," Chase said as he picked up his papers and stormed off onto the patio outside.

I looked up at Hazel and I could see mixed emotions spilling out of her. She just woke up to crazy bad news and an argument. "Tell me really why you don't want us to go kick some ass?" she demanded.

"I can't explain it to you, not right now, but I *do* know and you *both* have to trust me." I replied, trying to sound confident. "We will get captured and possibly killed if we go marching into their base," I added.

"Well, whatever you're not saying, you better think about saying it," she said. "Chase obviously spent a long time on this intel and you have to respect his effort and what he is bringing to the team. It's not good enough to say you *just know*. That's ridiculous!" Hazel then walked away and joined Chase on the patio. She even walked like she was mad, swinging her arms from side to side. I was mad too, but mostly at myself. I couldn't tell them about my visions yet and so there was no way to explain how I knew what was going to happen. This frustrated me. I knew what was going to happen but I couldn't change it. We were walking straight into a trap and I knew it. I felt powerless against time. If time and time again my visions were showing me what will

149

happen in the future I should take responsibility for it. But I can't take responsibility. Even though it is right in front of me I am unable to stop it from happening.

I was most afraid of losing my friends. Chase was pissed off at me and so was Hazel. How was I going to get them to cool down? I could try telling them about the glimpses of the future I have while I'm sleeping, but that just sounds crazy. They would probably just get more pissed off at me and think that I was just making excuses for being a know-it-all jerk. When this war is over, I thought, I'll tell them then. If it ends.

I picked up the papers and brought them to the light again. Just as before, the image on the top blended into the other paper easily. It was as if both of the images were made to be read together. I put the papers back down and reached for my spoon. There were only a few Cheerios left so I scooped them out and then washed out the bowl. I could hear my mom in my head telling me to drink the milk first, which I never did because the milk always contained soggy parts of the cereal which disgusted me. My eyes were tearing up though because I'd never *really* hear my mom's voice again.

On the table was Chase's bowl of cereal too. It was empty so I rinsed it along with mine. I owed him more than just rinsing his bowl for him. I was acting like an idiot when I insulted his plan and negated hours of his work. I put the bowls in the dishwasher and a terrible smell reminded me that I needed new clothes. So did Chase and Hazel. Maybe they would forget about this if I went out and spent some of my mom's money to get us all some clothes. I headed outside to find them.

I opened the door to find Chase and Hazel sitting there quietly watching the city. The outside air was begging me to come into its breeze. They looked up at me at the same time. "Hey," Hazel said, probably expecting me to apologize and explain myself.

"I stink," I said instead, trying to lighten the mood. "I was thinking I would go shopping for clothes. If you want anything, tell me." It was silent for a few seconds and I could tell they were thinking about what they would have me get. It worked.

"Just get me a few shirts, shorts, socks, and it would be great if I could get a toothbrush," Chase replied, breaking the ice.

I turned to Hazel expecting a request but she answered me differently. "I don't trust you to pick out my clothes," she said. "I'll go with you." When she stood up from her seat I noticed for the first time that we were pretty much the same height. And that meant we were both a couple inches taller than Chase.

"Sounds great! Let's get going then," I said cheerfully, trying to dissolve the tension between Chase and me.

Hazel sat back down to put on her shoes. "Hopefully Crofar isn't out buying clothes too," she said sarcastically as she slipped on both sneakers. She managed to get some laughter out of me but Chase was still in his moody state, except now he looked more concerned than mad. I guessed that he was worried Crofar might be out looking for us, or maybe that Crofar would find him at the house when no one else was there. One thing I knew about Chase was that even if he was mad, he still cared that we were all safe. That's what's so great about real friends. We may get into fights over stupid or unimportant things but in the end we are still friends. Taking a break from each other like this seemed like the right thing for Chase and me. Hazel walked next to me with less of a swing than before.

The morning was half over but we were making the best we could of the remaining hours. It was really great that we could just walk from our house to just about anywhere in the city. I walked fast hoping Hazel wouldn't want to talk about what just happened. I felt like a freak, or an alien. Maybe I had super-powers or maybe I was just psycho? Hazel wanted to know how I knew that Chase's plan wouldn't work but she seemed content to just ignore the topic entirely and continue walking. I was thankful that she did this. I didn't want her talking about Chase's plan. I needed a break.

"So," I stammered, suddenly uncomfortable with the silence, "what are you going to get in the clothing store?"

"Well, the usual stuff of course," she said running her hand down the length of her body, "but I would also love to get myself a jacket. I need something loose with pockets. What about you?"

"If you didn't notice already," I replied, lifting my arms, "I smell like a skunk. So I think I'm going to grab anything I can find." Hazel laughed at my answer and whatever tension was between us was gone. We were the same again.

"Did you know I could smell you from quite a distance?" Hazel asked, laughing. I started laughing along with her. A boy and a shirt attached for days is not a good thing. Our laughing settled down and then she said something that totally surprised me: "You're cute, John."

My mind was all over the place. From psycho-alien freak to cute--how does that happen? I felt like I had to tell her something nice and do it fast or she would think that I hated her. "Oh, thanks," I think I said, "You're beautiful. With or without new clothes." It came out so fast I didn't even have time to think about it.

Her cheeks quickly looked as if she had put on five pounds of blush. "Thanks," she said quietly. And the next thing I knew she was kissing me. I don't know if she ever felt this way before but I hadn't. And I was so glad I was the one who was with her now and not Chase. To be honest I had been a bit jealous whenever she hung out with Chase. I never really thought about what that meant until now. Maybe I liked Hazel more than I thought. And maybe she liked me too.

Thankfully our awkwardness was broken up because the store we were looking for was right in front of us. "Don't go on a spending spree, I'm begging you," I said handing her a wad of cash.

"Ha. I can't promise you anything," Hazel said and then rushed into the store ahead of me like she was on a hunt. She was moving so fast I thought she was going to get hit by a shopping cart or trip on her own shoelaces! I watched her disappear down an aisle of jeans and felt myself smiling, reliving that little kiss. Then the automatic doors beckoned me inside the cold air conditioned store, I grabbed a cart, and started to go down random aisles looking for clothes for Chase and me. Right away I found underwear and grabbed two packs for Chase and two packs for me. The whole area in the back was devoted to shoes. Little benches were being used by kids who were trying on shoes that lit up when they walked.

I never understood why kids were attracted to shoes that lit up but I decided to keep that to myself and ponder the answer at a different time. I walked through the store passing sections of many different styles of clothing. I then saw a table with layers of

155

shirts and shorts gathered in piles around it. I found our sizes and picked up four of each and threw them in the cart. Finally, I went to the toiletry section and grabbed a pink Sofia the First toothbrush for Chase and a plain blue one for me. It was time to look for Hazel.

I found an aisle with girls' jackets and I figured Hazel would be in there so I took a look around. I spotted her long brown hair lurking in front of a rack of sale items. She could hear me coming so she turned around. Her face was excited. "Check out this hellacious jacket I found!" Hazel raised her arms revealing the jacket she was talking about. The jacket was grey and it had holes in it. It was the same jacket she wore in the vision.

CHAPTER 15

"What's wrong?" Hazel asked. Her face transformed from cheerful to worry in a matter of seconds.

"Oh nothing," I deflected, "just thinking about the fight Chase and I had."

She seemed to buy this and continued on with her questioning. "Well, do you like the jacket?" Her question was so straightforward but it was a maze to me. If I told her not to get the jacket could it change the future? She wore that jacket like in my vision, so maybe if I got her to wear something else, I thought, we might not fall into the same trap. But how would a jacket affect the future? Only time would tell.

"That jacket looks like it was run over by a truck." I said, hoping my exaggeration would tilt her away from this jacket. "Wouldn't you rather get something that looks *new*?"

Hazel thought about this for a second. "Let me go grab another jacket and compare the two."

"Ok, but you better decide on one that looks like it cost something."

Hazel smiled and laughed to herself as she blended into the aisles of clothing. I looked around me and saw endless rows of female clothing. There were really short shorts, shirts that didn't cover your belly button, and many other things I couldn't understand why girls would ever want to wear. All this clothing reminded me of when I had to fold the laundry. If my clothes were next in line to be folded I was happy and wasn't grossed out. But when my mom's underwear and bras had to be folded I became a twitching freak. I always had to use the tip of my pointer finger and thumb like a claw to transport her clothes from one pile of unfolded laundry into a different one. My hands would flick her stuff off as fast as they could like I had a spider on my hand. I realized that I wouldn't have been grossed out if I had to fold her clothes now because I missed her so much.

While I waited for Hazel to return, thoughts of my old life were flooding into my brain. My mom would sing to my dad and

158

me all the time. Her singing could get a little off pitch but I would have done anything to hear her voice now. Her love for us was never ending. The way she protected me at the doctor's office was just one reminder of how much of a fighter she was for the ones she loved. She was incredibly tough. Many people say, "Like father, like son," but my mom and I had a special bond. I had thought nothing could ever split us apart. Nothing but the reality of her lying on the ground surrounded in her own blood. All I had left were these friends--Hazel and Chase--helping me stand up on my feet after that terrible scene. A tear rolled off my cheek and dripped down to my neck. I never expected that a sea of girls' clothing would bring back such memories.

Hazel made her way back to me loudly so I had a chance to wipe the tears from my neck and eyes. This time she had two jackets. "So which one do you like?" In her right hand she was holding a blue jacket with gold buttons. It looked way nicer than the one she was holding in her left hand: the grey one with holes.

"I like the blue jacket. It is way nicer and softer than the grey one." I said, thinking that would be the end of the grey jacket.

Hazel looked down at the two jackets she was holding. Her eyes moved from one jacket to the other comparing and contrasting both of them. I felt awkward having just cried about my parents and then standing there watching Hazel try to decide between two different jackets. She was still weighing the pros and cons in her head. I couldn't believe that if I didn't say anything about how bad the jacket with holes looked she would actually buy the thing without looking at different ones. I would rather get new clothes that looked new, rather than new clothes that looked like someone's hand-me-down. And what good is a jacket with holes in it anyway? "This is taking forever. Just pick one and let's go!" I said impatiently.

She tried each one on again while I stood there tapping my foot. "I think I'm going to go with the blue jacket," she finally conceded.

"Yessss," I said a little too loudly. For me the choice was obvious, but I also wanted to see what would change in the future if she didn't have that grey jacket with the holes in it.

Hazel was clearly annoyed. "Why are you so happy? You're not the one who has to wear it."

I couldn't help egging her on, even though I knew I was in dangerous territory. "It was just such an obvious decision," I said, grabbing the grey one out of her hand and putting it back on the rack.

Hazel looked confused at my response and defended herself. "It was such a hard decision! I had to make sure it was my style, type, and if it was comfortable." Then she brushed past me and made her way to the cashier. I looked down at my cart and contemplated the things I picked up earlier. Yep, this was all I needed so I followed Hazel to the front of the store.

It only took a few minutes for us to pay for our stuff and get out of the store. Hazel was walking ahead of me a little but she stopped and waited at the curb where we needed to turn to get home. "It's so nice outside," Hazel said, closing her eyes to feel the wind. She let her bag flap in the wind as she walked.

"Yeah it's great," I said, slowing down to make our walk together last as long as possible.

"Um...John?" she started. I looked at her, knowing what she was going to say. "That kiss we shared back there was really nice, but I just don't know if we should keep sharing those moments." Even though I saw this statement coming it still hit me in the chest like a knife. A weird mixture of love and sadness and resolve showed on her face. I felt them too. "I really like you," she continued, "but things are pretty scary right now and we've got to stay focused on defeating the T.F.G., or at least escaping their fate for us. Plus, I don't want to make Chase feel bad. I know I give him a lot of crap, but he's really a good guy. Don't tell him I said so."

My face became cold and the winds became stronger. I loved that thing we had for a second, but she was right. We were at war with the T.F.G. and things could go to hell fast. Right now is not the best time to start any relationship beyond friendship and the fact that Hazel brought this up right away made me realize that she was smarter than I had given her credit for. "It sucks to say this but you're right," I replied.

I had no idea what else to say. I couldn't try to talk my way around this relationship ban because, well, she *was* right. I looked for her to weaken her resolve but she showed no emotion at all. That's the big problem with being in a relationship during times like these. Just a little movement on her face could send me running in the wrong direction. She knew that.

"Once we bring down the T.F.G., if we do, it would be great to start something with you John," she added. We stopped in our tracks and faced each other. My heart was pounding and a smile grew on her face. As gently as possible, I leaned in. My eyes closed just like Hazel's had when she breathed in the wind. But now she was breathing in me and I was breathing in her. Her hair whipped around our faces shielding us from the world. The bags we carried fell to the ground. Her hands rested on my arms and her fingers pressed lightly into my skin. Right as she touched me, nothing could hurt me. I was finally locked away from death and the T.F.G. Locked away from wars, fights, and hate. Locked away from everything except for this one person, Hazel. I was wishing that I could choose a superpower. If I could choose, I would have chosen the ability to freeze time. This moment was so perfect and I was so glad that Hazel had ignited this spark between us. I had saved her but she was saving me too. I felt her hands slowly reach up to my neck. Everywhere she touched my nerves were tingling.

She drew her face back from mine and looked at me, smiling. "You're such a sweet guy, John. John…what?"

I smiled back at her and took in every line and detail of her face. Who knows when we would be this close again. "Williams," I told her. "I am John Williams."

"Thank you for everything you have done to help me and Chase, Mr. Williams." she said as she bowed her head slightly. "We are forever in your debt."

"Anything for my two favorite friends." I responded, bowing my head in return. "Well, my *only* friends."

Her smile grew even bigger. The wind was gently rushing through us and she decided to leave me with one more gentle kiss before she stepped back. Her hands drew down my arms and rested to her sides. She tilted her head to the side and reminded us both that this was only a moment, "I can't wait to know you better after all this fighting ends."

It was another gut punch but I was glad she said it. "And I can't wait for that too," I replied, feeling my stomach churn. "We can still hang and stuff, right?" I asked her.

"Right," Hazel said sharply, almost like nothing had happened. "Shall we get going?"

I picked up all of the bags and we started walking, falling easily back into our usual outward focus on the streets and the people, scanning for odd occurrences. Now we knew that right below us was the T.F.G.'s headquarters so we had to be especially careful. We didn't speak again the whole way home. Hazel seemed to be deep in thought, or just enjoying nature--I couldn't tell. I was thinking about her jacket.

Could something really this small have a big effect on the future? Just a change of color and change of texture might have enough power to *do* something? I had never been afraid of sleeping, as it was always my most favorite hobby, but seeing what the future holds during my only snooze time is just a little unnerving. Dreams had also been welcomed by me, especially when I dreamt about fighting a huge dinosaur or taking over the world. But now I had to dream about reality--or future reality--and I was kind of dreading it.

I tried to focus on the world I was in now. To my left were shops and restaurants urging customers to buy their items using signs, sales, and gimmicks. A sign read "10% off!" Ten percent off of what, I wondered. It could be something that costs thousands of dollars or ten dollars. Either way, that tiny sale would not induce me to buy something I didn't need.

To my right was Hazel, more stunning than ever, looking out into the streets. Her eyes were set on buildings that engulfed the area around it. Buildings towered over anything that tried to be larger. It was all so quiet and stationary. There were no groups of people, no shouts, no parades, no bustle, and there were no T.F.G. soldiers. There was just the breeze I had felt this morning and a lifelessness I had not noticed before.

Where I used to live we had houses with gardens. Plants expanded beyond the front yard as if each flower was trying to show off to all the other flowers. We had greenery and blue skies and cookies when we got home from school. There was also life in our neighborhood that spilled over into my home. Sure it was quiet but it was never that quiet. Kids from all around the neighborhood biked up and down the long rows of homes seeking adventure. Now I realize they were seeking time away from their mute parents. I would stand there on my porch looking out at their glowing faces. I wanted now to help them with their journeys, to keep them safe, and tell them what had been going on all this time. Yet, I really couldn't help them. I was powerless now and I always had been.

All of this made me crazy. I was powerless to save all those kids in the clinic. I was powerless to save my parents. I felt powerless to stop Hazel from getting shot, even though I *knew* it was going to happen. I *saw* it happen. I couldn't change *anything!* The last time I checked there was no cure to craziness. But there was a mental aid for me. There was Hazel. She was my only cure but I felt powerless again because we couldn't start a relationship until all of this was over but I didn't know if it would ever be over, or if I could make it that long. Maybe all I had to look forward to a few hidden kisses.

"Hey what's going on? You look a million miles away," Hazel beckoned as we walked. She snapped me back from my gloomy trance and I was determined not to take her down with me.

"Nothing," I said, "It's just the weather. The wind is bothering me." I immediately knew I should have chosen a different gripe because the weather was actually pretty nice. In fact, it couldn't have been more refreshing to be outside.

"The wind is bothering you? You mean this soft breeze is the thing that is making you annoyed and quiet? Come on, John, you can't seriously think I'm that dumb. What is going on?" Hazel demanded.

"I don't think you're dumb, Hazel. It's just that with everything going on recently, it is too much to handle sometimes for me," I said, releasing the bags I was carrying to my fingertips.

Hazel seemed to understand. She relented anyway, at least for a few minutes. But then she turned to me, looking very serious. "John," she said, "if it's me, or kissing me, or me kissing you, or not kissing, will you tell me?"

There was no way I was going to let her think it was her fault. "What?! No! Hazel, I am not talking about us. *You* are amazing and *we* are good. I can't stop thinking about my visions!"

Yes, I blurted that out in one stupid breath. I couldn't believe that the word "visions" escaped my mouth. I thought, *There is no cure for craziness. Is there? Nope. Not for me. I will never change back to the John I used to be.*

"Visions?" Hazel asked, looking sort of incredulous. "What do you mean, *visions?*"

I stood there dumbfounded. I couldn't speak. My brain was racing for a way to pull this one out, but I could come up with nothing.

"Come on, John, answer me. You know you can't stay this way forever."

"Fine," I said, hoping surly would mask my lie. "I am having nightmares. Visions of bad memories, like my parents dying. It's making me a little insane. I even fell off my bed and hurt myself." I added a sniffle to emphasize my emotional pain. Acting was never my strong suit but I didn't really need to act--I *was* going a little insane and I *did* hurt myself.

"I'm sorry, John. I didn't mean to bring that up. If you suffer from another nightmare, I wouldn't mind if you came into my room and woke me up," she offered.

That went better than I hoped. "Thanks," I said, and we left it at that. Soon enough the daylight dimmed and our house rose in the shadows. When we were close enough to see its edges I stopped and looked behind me to see the lights of the city.

"Never look back," Hazel advised as she took my hand and gently pulled me toward the house. When we reached the bottom of the porch stairs I asked Hazel for one more kiss. "You beggar!" she joked as she granted me my wish.

Time always moves and perfect moments don't last, no matter how hard you try. I pulled back slightly and looked into her eyes. Bright blue with speckles of brown surrounded dark pupils. Hazel looked right back at me as we tried to make the moment last. But something over her shoulder caught my eye.

Something was on the porch--it was barely visible but I knew it wasn't there before. It looked like a tiny camera. "Hazel," I whispered, "be quiet and don't look just yet. Someone is watching us through that small lump on the porch." Hazel raised her eyebrows and gulped. She turned around and we walked up the steps of our house trying not to seem shaken. I got behind the camera and motioned for her to join me. From there we could see that the camera was tightly connected to the porch and was painted the same color as the wood.

I handed the bags over to Hazel so I could break the camera. I was about to kick it with my shoe when Chase burst through the front door. "Whoa, whoa, whoa, karate kid, what do you think you're doing?" he asked. Then he gestured to the camera tucked into the porch railing. "This is *ours*! It's our eyes and ears--now we can know what's going on outside before it comes inside, get it?"

Hazel and I looked at Chase with surprise. "Oh, gosh," I said, wondering if he was just watching us kissing by the porch. "Where did you get it?"

"Well, while you two were *out*," he said, glaring at me, "I got a visit from the guy from the Renegades. He basically said that we were joining forces and that we needed this camera so they could help us if we needed it."

"And you *trusted* him?" I said, a bit too obnoxiously.

"Do we have a choice?" Chase shot back. "Look, if we are in trouble they will help us as long as we respect them and keep their identity a secret, and if they are in trouble and can use our help, we will come to their aid," Chase explained. "So to answer your question, yeah, I thought that was reasonable."

"I think that's great!" Hazel said, looking at me like I was being a ridiculous jerk.

171

I felt like crawling into a hole. "Yeah. Thanks man," I choked out as I offered him a fist-bump. "But how will they know if we are in trouble?"

He looked back at the camera. "They have access to this camera, as we do. I can view this camera through a link on the laptop that is highly secured. I sent them the link and how to get through the system. If we go inside I will show you," Chase offered.

We headed inside and Hazel set the bags on the kitchen table and wandered back to her room. Chase and I walked over to his laptop with its screen broadcasting our front porch to the Renegades. I had many reasons to be worried about this camera but one was really bothering me. "Hooking up with a fierce chick? I don't understand your taste in girls," Chase quipped. I responded quietly, "You saw me kiss Hazel?" "Unfortunately, yes. You guys kiss like a dog and a toad," Chase laughed at his own remark. I can't lie, I smirked a bit too.

CHAPTER 16

Relieved, I changed the subject. "How is the camera connected to the laptop?" I asked.

"The camera communicates remotely though this little USB stick," Chase explained, pointing to the square thing sticking out of the side of his laptop. I pretended to be interested in Chase's camera set-up but I was really distracted by Hazel who had come back from her room and was searching through the bags of clothing. I could tell she wasn't interested in the camera, but I could also tell that she was mad at me for not including her.

Chase seemed oblivious to everything except the laptop screen. It was like he was hypnotized by it. I stared at the screen too. I could see the front porch illuminated from the outdoor lighting. I could see faint lights from the edge of the city too, but the porch light was bright and sparkling. This was an advantage, I started to think, and having advantages such as this would be the key to winning this war. Sure the T.F.G. had an underground base, but they would have to come up this porch to get to us.

I looked up to see what Hazel was doing but she was nowhere to be seen. I thought she was probably in her room so I looked back at the screen, but instead of seeing the porch from the camera, there was nothing. Something was blocking our view-- and it was moving. Soon enough I realized that it was Hazel--she was outside on the porch, at first blocking the view with her body and then backing up to wave at the camera. She started moving her lips to say something but no sound was coming out of the laptop. I looked at Chase in confusion. He looked back at me with the same expression. "You said it had a mic, right?" I asked him.

"Yeah it does. I just don't know why it is not working." Chase pushed me to the side so he could work on the laptop. He clicked around like a pro but we could both see the volume control was all the way up. "This doesn't make sense," he said, "the sound was working when I bought it."

Hazel was still looking at us from the screen but she was no longer waving--she was motioning us to come outside. "What does she want?" Chase asked, looking up at me with a dumb look.

"I don't know but whenever she needs us it is for a good reason," I responded.

Chase sighed and stood up. I followed him to the door and we went outside to see Hazel standing there in front of the camera. "We are kinda busy right now so what do you need?" Chase asked, emphasizing his irritation.

She pointed to the camera, carefully tucked into the porch rail and painted brown to blend in. "*That* is why I wanted you to come out here. Don't you think that covering the back of the camera with paint will, you know, *ruin* it," she quipped.

"*Ruin it?* The sound is not working. Paint wouldn't affect the sound," Chase said, so sure of himself.

"Uh. What I am trying to make you realize is that you covered the microphone with paint. That's why you can't hear anything on it," she responded, giving Chase the *you-idiot* look.

Chase's face lit up as he processed the information, and then turned a little red. He walked over to the camera and dug his fingernail into the side of the camera and chipped off some of the paint. "Man, how dumb am I?"

"Yeah, duh!" I said, ribbing him for his little oversight.

"I didn't see you figuring it out," Chase said quietly as he examined the camera's mic. I started laughing and he grinned. "There we go. I got all the paint off the mic. Hazel, say something to the camera. I'm going to see if it works."

I followed him back inside and we both leaned over the laptop. Hazel was back in position facing the camera. "You're welcome, by the way," we could hear her saying. We then watched Hazel turn around and walk towards the door. A creek coming from our front door made its way to our ears. We looked behind us to see Hazel walking towards us. "Did it work?" she asked.

"Yup," I told her, expecting a big smile to appear on her face any second. I was definitely wrong about that. Instead, she bit her bottom lip, walked up to me and slapped my face. Then she went right over to Chase and did the same. A small sting on my cheek grew and Chase and I looked at each other wondering what the hell that was for.

"What the hell was that for?!" I heard myself say out loud.

She looked at me like my mom used to when I didn't know what lesson she was teaching. "Don't you mean to say, *thank you?*" she asked.

I opened my mouth to apologize but she stormed off into her room. "Ouch," Chase said, rubbing his very red cheek and looking at mine. "I thought you two had something going on!"

Chase's remark had me shaking my head. I didn't know what was going on with Hazel. Before I could make some smart-ass response he was up and rummaging through our shopping bags on the table. "We got you some clothes," I said.

"Thanks," Chase said, as he began searching the bags for his clothes. "*What the...?*"

"What now?" I responded.

"*The hell, dude?!*" Chase yelled as he held up the toothbrush I got him. I started cracking up as Chase repeated, "Not funny, dude! *Not funny!*"

I grabbed the bags and threw out Chase's clothes so I could take mine to my room. I was headed to my room still laughing when a noise diverted my attention. I heard crying coming from Hazel's room. I threw the clothes in my room and stood at the door of her room wondering what I should do. In a minute or two it sounded like she was over the climax of her crying and just sniffling. I knocked lightly and slowly opened the door to her room, figuring she would stop me if she wanted to be alone. She was sitting on her bed with her hands over her eyes. Her bedroom was almost identical to mine except it had her things strewn across the floor. She didn't look up at me so I decided to go to her. Tears were falling from her hands. I sat next to her and wrapped my arms around her. She dropped her hands from her eyes and let herself fall into me.

"Why are you crying?" I asked.

Her face burrowed into my chest and her arms tightened around my body. She was able to speak but her voice was shaky and she kept stopping to catch her breath. "You and Chase are.... great but.... I can never really be close to both of you. You guys.... have always been best buds... and I just tag along but.... I will never be as close.... to you as you guys are already....and I am scared."

I held her firmly while she calmed down. "Please don't worry about that," I said. "Yeah, Chase and I are close--I mean, we've been friends for a long time--but we are all in this together now and I trust you like I've never trusted anyone before. And I *want* us to be close--as close as we can be in this messed up T.F.G.

world." I brushed her hair to the side of her face and her softness and vulnerability took me by surprise. Hazel always seemed so tough, like she was the one that would lead us through this. I wanted her to feel her own strength again. "Besides," I continued, "we have to be pretty close already--you did just slap us both in the face!"

"You deserved it!" Hazel said, letting out a little laugh and then softening again. "Thank you, John. I guess this is the opposite of me helping you."

We both smiled and held each other again, but this time it was more like a hug. I stood up and tried to think of something casual to say. "Do you think you can get some sleep?" I asked. "Maybe we'll be able to sleep in if Chase stays up late enough."

"Goodnight, John," she whispered, "You are my knight."

"Goodnight, Hazel," I said and crossed the hall into my room. I was still a little confused about why she was so upset but I was glad that it happened like that. I did feel closer to her, and I wanted to be closer still.

The clothes I had put in my room were lying on the floor on top of one another. At the bottom of the stack was my wallet.

I picked up the clothes, tried them on, ripped off the tags, and put them away. I was surprised how comfortable everything fit, and how cheap this stuff was. My mom would have been proud.

My bed was waiting for me to join it so I did. "Here we go," I thought to myself as I pulled the blanket over me. I was ready to see what changes might occur in tonight's dream. I would soon know if changing something in the present did anything to the future. My room was dark and I tried to clear my mind from all thoughts and images. Instead I thought about how it used to make me sad to see darkness take over light; how I always tried to stretch out the day as much as I could. Then I imagined my memories and distractions being shoved into a garbage bag in my head and tossed into space. The only image I allowed in my head was the color red. Red was my favorite color. I closed my eyelids and saw this color bloom in front of me like a sunflower blossoming in the summer. Except the flower was all red and so was the background. The only thing I saw then, this redness, relaxed me and made me want to be one with it. The color moved and stretched and got brighter and then darker, pulsating on the inside of my eyelids. Soon enough the color turned into an image, and then a scene, and then...

I was back in the vision. Two shots busted my ears from in front of me. I opened my eyes to see what was going on. Hazel stood in front of me with a gun in her hand. "Wow, they totally cleared your memory," someone said to my right.

I was still recovering from jumping into the dream but I remembered Chase saying this in my last vision. "I thought you apologized for saying that," I said to him. These words came out of my mouth without me even saying them.

"Oh yeah my bad," Chase responded, just like before. Sirens were exploding from the ceiling and flashing lights accompanied them. I was in the past living in the future.

"There's about a dozen soldiers turning the corner ahead," Hazel yelled back at us. Everything was exactly the same as the last vision except Hazel looked different this time. This time she was wearing a blue jacket with golden buttons. Chase was staring at something in front of us so I followed his stare. Of course, as I had seen before, there were twelve T.F.G. soldiers with guns looking at us. Hazel handed me a knife and said, "This is going to be a hell of a fight."

I opened my mouth to say ok but I was not in control. I felt something odd happen to my mouth. It opened itself and out came the words, "A knife?! They all have guns!"

"Is Chase complaining?" Hazel asked in annoyance, as expected.

My mouth was shutting itself and there was no way I could stop it. I tried to tell her to watch out when she runs back but I couldn't. My own mouth didn't let me. The knife Hazel gave me was exactly like the knife she handed me before. It was matte black with shapes entangling and overlapping each other. The logo Amber Arms was spread out on its side. T.F.G. soldiers were looking at us waiting for a move to be made. Hazel slowly reached down to her jacket and took out another gun. *No holsters this time*, I thought. My body ached as I wanted to pull her to cover but I was paralyzed on the inside. I couldn't move or talk. History was being made and time didn't want me to change it. Hazel jolted her arms into the air, holding two guns. Bullets flew through the air and three soldiers dropped down to the floor dead.

Something seemed off about her shots. In the last vision she shot and hit soldiers but there was more recoil. I focused on one of the guns she was holding and it was definitely a gun that I had not seen before. The only detail I could make out on the gun was a faint logo in the shape of a circle. Also, I recalled two soldiers dropping when she shot at them, not three. All of us ran to the side of the wall because the T.F.G. members started to shoot at us with their assault rifles. It was really hard for me to process that I wasn't trying to run over to the wall, yet I was at the same time running to the wall.

Chase and I stood behind Hazel who kept firing at the soldiers. Her gun was firing at a rate that was a lot faster than her old gun. After a few moments of sirens and shooting my body peeked around the corner to see how many men she had killed. There were six soldiers remaining, which was incredible. They took cover and started firing their guns at anything they could.

In a barrage of gunfire, Hazel started to sprint for cover too. Bullets spun past her body but this time she made it to cover safely. My nerves started coming back to their senses. I felt my hands coming back to use, and also my mouth. Since Hazel didn't get shot, everything from this point forward would be new to me. "Hey, take this," Hazel said to me as she handed me one of her guns. As she reloaded the gun in her hand, the sirens came to a stop. This happened in the last vision too, except this time Hazel and I had switched places. The only distraction left was the bright flashing light on the ceiling.

Once she finished reloading the gun, I quickly handed her the one I was holding. It felt great to be able to move and talk again. Being trapped in a body that was moving without my consent was daunting and I didn't want to face that again. Shots kept hitting the walls around us, grazing the floor and the ceiling and bouncing off metal doors. The T.F.G. soldiers were not about to give up. There was so much gunfire, it would have been almost impossible for Hazel to fire back. "You can't turn that corner safely," I said to her, fearing she would try anyway.

She stared down at me almost smiling saying, "Once we have a *real* relationship, you can start worrying about me." I smiled back at her knowing that we did have a real relationship. My mom would have said that we were too young but I was thinking we were adults since we pretty much had the weight of the world on us at that point. I missed my mom more than anything. I had no time to mourn her loss and just think about her. Still, I couldn't exactly convince my two friends to hold back on our attempt at saving the world.

Hazel turned around the corner to fire back and I watched her go down. Again I felt out of control as my feet carried my body to where she was as fast as they could go. I dragged her back behind the corner. "Are you ok?" I asked her as I checked every inch of her to see where she was shot. My heart panicked and all I could think about was losing her. My hands lifted her and moved her to see where she had been punctured with a bullet.

I kept searching but I could find no blood. "John I'm fine," she said. "I didn't get shot. The wall shook and it knocked me off my feet. Really I'm ok."

"The wall shook?" I asked her. I was hoping that it wasn't caused by the endless army of soldiers from my last vision. Maybe changing the jacket would have some little effect on the future but it was not enough to change our fate.

"Yeah, it was like a bomb had hit it," she explained.

"We need to run and get out of here," I told Hazel as I lifted her up. "Chase, we need to leave now!"

"Where are we going to go?" Chase wanted to know. "The exit is past the T.F.G. dudes, that way," he finished, pointing in the direction of the gunfire.

"Yeah, well our lives are the other way. Move now!" I demanded, pushing them both with my hands in the direction I wanted them to go. They started to run and I followed. Chase had a knife in his hand that had the same logo as Hazel's new guns. The lights pulsated and our shadows bounced around, disappearing and reappearing all around us, like a dance with many more people. We passed several offices but no one was in them. The hallway seemed to go on forever in this gigantic T.F.G. base. The walls had stopped shaking but that could have been from our distance from the action, or, whatever was hitting the walls had stopped altogether. We ran and ran and then there was nowhere to run. "Damn it," I yelled, pounding my fists on the wall at the end of an endless maze of hallways.

"Looks like you led us in the wrong direction, I mean if we wanted to *live*," Chase said in an *I told you so* kind of way.

"Not helpful, Chase!" I screamed, "We better the hell find an office to hide in!" I was really mad at Chase, probably because I was afraid he might be right.

"I see one. Follow me," Hazel said, sprinting in the direction of a door we had already passed. Chase and I followed her without question. Hazel opened the door and let us inside. There were no sirens or blinking lights inside of this office, which was very helpful in the drained state we were all in. The office door had a big window, giving us few hiding spots, but it was high enough for us to crouch below it and we each did so instinctively.

The office was big with a long desk stretching across the heart of it. I noticed many papers scattered on top of it. "Wait here," I said to Chase and Hazel, "I'm going to see if I can get any information from that pile of stuff on the desk."

"No don..." Hazel tried to stop me but she gave up when she could see I was going anyway. We could hear noises outside the door so I knew I had to be fast and keep my head down. I reached the desk and lowered my body behind it, with my head just enough above it to see what was on top. Some of the papers were folded and I couldn't read them, but a newspaper did catch my eye. There was an article in the Amber Daily about the shot clinic:

Three teenagers wanted for terrible crimes

Three teenagers are wanted for setting a Grand Sile clinic on fire. Those that survived the disaster were left with burns and injuries. The teens are thought to be in hiding in Amber and are considered armed and dangerous. If you have information about their whereabouts, call 911. Information that leads to their apprehension is subject to a $10,000 reward.

Another article on the same page was about a gas leak, but I didn't have time to read it. I shoved the page into my pocket. The sounds from outside got louder and louder, so I quickly crawled on all fours back to my friends. "What did you take?" Chase asked me.

"A newspaper article," I replied. "Three armed and dangerous teenagers are wanted for setting a clinic on fire. Ten thousand bucks if you turn us in!" Hazel looked at me with fire in her eyes. I reached out to hold her hand in mine and squeezed it tightly. Things were suddenly very quiet outside the door, and Chase was looking at me very worried. "Okay," I whispered, "I'm going to see what's going on outside this office."

"Since when have you become so independent?" Hazel asked.

"Since I was born," I replied, puffing myself up for a terrifying peek into our future.

Outside the office an army of heavily armed men waited, as I expected. It struck me though that they weren't wearing the usual T.F.G. soldiers' uniform. These guys were wearing dark clothes and ski masks. Maybe they were some special unit, I thought. There were enough men and gear on them to end this little battle in minutes. The men were quietly checking every office looking for us. Shortly they were going to open the door of the office that we are hiding in. We were as good as dead.

I lowered my head to the height of Chase's and Hazel's and told them the truth: "The soldiers are searching the offices for us so we are pretty much dead. Any last words?"

"What?! I am not saying any last words. I am going to make a move," Hazel responded. In less than a heartbeat she had opened the door and stepped out into the hallway. I was dumbfounded.

"*What* is she doing?" Chase said, not expecting an answer. We both rose to the window and looked out into the hall. I briefly stopped breathing.

"I don't know what she thinks she's doing and I don't like it, but she is usually one step ahead of us so whatever she's doing, it better work," I said. We watched Hazel approach and then start talking to the men wearing the ski masks. They surrounded her and she continued to speak, pointing and explaining, and holding their attention. I couldn't figure out what was going on. Why were they listening to her? Just then, one of the masked men turned toward Chase and I and caught sight of us through the window of our hiding spot. The man pulled off his mask and smiled. I couldn't believe it. It was Maximus, the leader of the Renegades.

CHAPTER 17

My eyes opened to see my room around me. I couldn't believe that I had been running from my allies. I had to process this new version of the future and there's nothing like a shower for focused thinking.

I jumped out of bed and went to the bathroom. Inside of our simple Amber rental home bathroom was a sink, a toilet, and a shower. I flipped the light switch on and the flickering bulb momentarily scared me. It was like a flashback to the T.F.G. showdown and I immediately turned off the lights, realizing that I was still going to have go through that nightmare in real life. I also realized that even though the Renegades came to save us, I was still not sure how we got out of there, or even that we did. It was still a possibility, for all I knew, that not only would our mission fail, but we ended up dead.

I got into the shower and turned the water on full blast. Freezing cold water sputtered and then drenched me as I jumped out of the way and waited for it to warm. The darkness in this tiny space was worse than the flickering light so I reached out of the shower and felt around for the light switch. My hands were shaking a little. Not being able to see things had always scared me. But for the past three days I had been able to see the future and that scared me even more. The thing that really scared me was that what I was seeing could be changed and I didn't know how things would change or what would change them. It seemed like seeing the future was no better than not seeing the future.

My mom used to tell me that sometimes the things you can't bear are the things that make you thrive. The light bulb on the ceiling flickered to life and I closed my eyes, clutching the walls for anything to help me find some balance. Living through my future every night was depriving me of sleep and I felt like hope was the only thing pushing me forward. Soon my friends and I would see how this standoff really ends.

I grabbed the bar of soap and let the steaming hot water pour over me. I had to think. I remembered the newspaper that I

192

put into my pocket in the vision and my mind was instantly flooded with questions. *When will that article be written? Was it already written? The T.F.G. must have written the newspaper article because nobody else would know that we were in Amber. Why would the T.F.G. write newspaper articles if everyone was mind-controlled by Crofar and his army? Maybe the newspapers are part of how the T.F.G. controls people's minds. The article also said that some people escaped from the building. Could my dad have survived? It would be the most helpful and hopeful thing to me if my dad was still alive. No, that would be impossible.*

I finished scrubbing myself clean and I let the hot water rain on me for a few more minutes. I was comfortable and happy there but I knew it couldn't last. Even if we win this war, I thought, my parents wouldn't be there to celebrate our victory. It was a sinking thought but I didn't let it sink me. We had to win. We just had to win. I opened the shower door and stepped onto the cold floor and into a steam chamber. I grabbed the big towel on the rack and wrapped it around myself like I used to do at home every morning. I stopped in front of the sink's mirror and saw a fuzzy replica of myself. I rubbed off a little square of steam and what looked like an older version of myself stared back at me.

His straight brown hair was a little too long and his serious face was framed with thick dark eyebrows and a squarish jaw. He only vaguely resembled the little boy that always wanted to do what was right but sometimes broke the rules. It scared me how much I had changed in this short time and I knew there was no going back.

My feet froze as I stepped outside the bathroom. I walked fast into my room and threw on some of my new clothes. I was starving so I hurried into the kitchen still pulling my shirt over my head. Chase was eating cereal in front of the laptop. I felt safe knowing that he was determined to make sure that no one set foot on our porch. "Thanks for keeping watch," I said to Chase.

He looked up briefly and scanned me up and down. He refrained from commenting on whatever he noticed. "I can't let anyone barge in on the best kids in the world," he said, and then turned up the enthusiasm. "Did you know that the camera has night vision?"

"Geez, the Renegades got some nice gear," I replied, trying to meet his excitement. It was weird talking about the group of people that only I knew were going to save us when Chase's plan goes south. Chase went back to staring at his screen while I opened the cabinets to see what we had to eat. On the first shelf was our last box of chocolate pop tarts.

"I can't believe you didn't eat these!" I said, ridiculously happy to see my favorite food in the house.

"They're all yours!" Chase said, laughing. He was clearly delighted that he had saved them for me.

"You're the best, man," I replied, ripping into the box like I was a man on the brink of starvation. I took out two chocolate covered pop tarts and put them in the toaster. "You're not expecting friends to come over, are you?"

"I agree with you," Chase said, standing up and stretching his arms over his head. It was everything he could do to not sit right back down and watch that damn screen. "Even though it's important to be on the lookout, I think we should all go somewhere outside today," he said, "I was thinking that we should get new weapons and train for the mission tomorrow."

I thought about this for a minute and since I didn't want to screw up the timeline, I had to follow everything I thought we probably did before what I had seen of the future in my visions.

But I was also worried about that newspaper article. People in Amber would be on the lookout for us. "That sounds great," I said reluctantly, knowing that we were going to need to get the weapons that I had seen in my last vision. "But where are we going to train with our new weapons?" I asked.

"Yeah, that's going to be a problem," Chase admitted, "especially since we are basically sitting on top of the T.F.G. base. Scrap the plan about training. We still need weapons though."

"That's for sure," I offered. "When do you want to go?"

Chase moved away from the laptop and poured himself another bowl of Cheerios. "I guess we go when Hazel wakes up, like a day or so from now," he said, sounding a little exasperated about how late Hazel was sleeping in.

Rapid beeping from the toaster told me that my pop tarts had popped up. I took a plate and tossed the scorching hot rectangles of breakfast perfection on it and watched one of them skid off the other side. I picked it up carefully so it wouldn't crumble and whisked the plate over to the table where Chase was covering his bowl of Cheerios in milk. "Can't wait to swallow this down whole," I told Chase as I made myself comfortable at the table.

"Go for it. See how much I care," he responded nonchalantly as he turned his head toward the laptop screen so he could eat and watch the porch.

"Wow! Look how much our front patio has changed!" I chided him again, accidentally nudging the arm that was holding a spoonful of Cheerios that was on its way to his mouth. The spoon was like a catapult and the target was his face. I tried to cover up my laugh as he processed what had happened, but his stunned expression made me laugh even harder. Finally he turned his milk-dampened face towards me, picked up his bowl and launched its entire contents right at me. Milk was the only thing I saw before I was covered in it.

"Come on man," I squeaked out, "I just showered and put on new clothes!"

"Hope you learned your lesson," Chase replied, looking pleased with himself.

Next to me were my pop tarts ready to be eaten. I picked one up and dipped it into the milk pooling in the folds of my shirt. Then I took a big bite exaggerating my chewing for Chase. His lips curved down in disgust. "That's nasty," he said.

I managed a smile as I walked to my room. I was thinking that just this morning I had seen a man staring back at me in the mirror, only to be reduced to this milk-soaked boy by my best friend. And I didn't have so many new clothes that I could afford another change! I looked at the piles of clothes in my room and suddenly felt like a man again, this time surveying that kid's room. *What a mess.* In my hand was my drenched t-shirt. My pants were another victim of the milk scene. Straight ahead were old clothes piled on one another. They were screaming, "Mess!" Accompanying the chorus were my bed sheets, curled at the bottom of my bed. This was a pigsty and it had to change. Unfortunately, it was my pigsty and I had to change it.

I began picking up the clothes and organizing them. I folded everything, even the dirty disgusting things I had been wearing for days. Just like I had done for years, I took the shirts and folded the arms in first. Then I carefully wrapped the two sides of the shirt in on itself. The last thing to be done was to fold it in half. I learned this not from my mom, but from my dad. I

forehead, released his grasp and studied me. The smile on his face died and he looked stressed and worried. At the time I had no sense of what he was feeling but I had come to realize that he loved me more than he could show. To show my love in return I needed to keep that promise. *Was I capable of keeping that promise?*

I turned to the bed to make it, but something else caught my attention. Lying on the bedside table was the wallet my mom had given me. Its brown outer shell enhanced an odd circular shape. I ran my fingers along the pattern and then opened it. The wallet was filled with cash and photos. I pulled out the photos and put three of them on the floor side by side. In one, I was smiling at the camera from inside the pool. My mom was sitting on the chair watching me. It was a sunny day and light bounced off the bottom of the pool. My dad must have taken that one. In the next photo I was leaning against an exterior wall of our house. My hair was all messed up from the wind. The last photo was of the whole family. All of us stood smiling in front of a brick wall. This wall was part of the alleyway near our house. I remembered when we took this photo. My body shivered a bit just thinking about it. A flash was used because the alleyway was dark. My dad clicked the ten second button and then ran towards us. He took the left side of me and immediately stared at the camera. We sat there silently and patiently waiting for the camera to blind us with its flash.

Seeing these pictures was like a knife in the heart. I missed them so much. That feeling of loss was almost constant, especially when it was quiet. I couldn't bear looking at the photos anymore so I put them back in the wallet. As I closed the wallet something poked out from the side of it. It was the jump drive. Instantly I pulled it out. I couldn't believe that I had forgotten about it. We had bought the laptop for a reason but I had been so caught up in my visions that I had forgotten about what we were supposed to be doing with it. I ran into the kitchen and shoved the jump drive into the laptop. The chair was still crooked from when I got hit with milk so I straightened it and sat down. I waited for the new drive to load and then I scrolled through all of the files on the drive, hoping to see one that seemed meant for me. About half way down I found a file called "Love you." I opened it. It was a letter from my mom.

CHAPTER 18

Dear John,

If you're reading this, it is likely that I have passed away. But it means that helping you escape the T.F.G.'s "vaccination" was a success. Before you read anymore please make sure that no one else is reading this with you, not even your dad. It is meant only for you.

My eyes stopped at the word, "dad." It was difficult enough reading a note from my mother whom I knew I would never see again. It was even harder reading about my dad in her note to me. Of course she had no idea that both of them would die protecting me. At this point she didn't know that Chase and Hazel are with me either. *When did she write this? How long did she plan this escape before it happened? Did she know she wouldn't make it?* With these questions in mind, I read on.

I don't want to make this too hard on you but I just have to say that I love you to the end of the universe and back. Your dad also loves you much more than you realize. I really hope that you see his love and compassion for you as you move forward without me. We are both super proud of you but no one could be as proud of you as I am. I am so honored and lucky to have you as my son and wish that I could have had more memories and experienced more of your extraordinary life.

I don't want you to ever forget me. I will always be alive as long as you remember. That is why I put some photos in the wallet, along with some money to help get you through. One of the photos is from a day we all went out for ice cream. Remember when we were at the ice cream shop after school and you got a chocolate cone and your dad and I got a vanilla sundae? You sat down to wait for your ice cream and dad and I told the server to fill the bottom of the cone with water and put the ice cream on top. When we handed you the booby-trapped cone it was hard to contain our laughter. We sat down eating our vanilla sundaes while watching you and waiting for you to finish the ice cream in the cone. You took a bite out of the bottom of the cone and water came shooting out of the sides of the cone and splashed all over your shirt. The look on your face was priceless and my cheeks hurt from laughing. I don't want you to forget the happy memories we have made as a family.

Now, here is the important part. There is almost no one that you can trust out there in the world. The T.F.G. is powerful and ruthless and their numbers increase all the time as more and more people get their shots. Even your dad cannot be trusted if he has been given this shot. Look for signs before you decide to trust anyone. Anyone! There is a group of fighters called the Renegades--they live in that creepy alley in the walls--and you can trust them. How do I know that you get scared whenever you walk home from school in that alley? They tell me.

Even though I just said you could trust them, always use your own judgment because it's possible they could make a bad decision, or the T.F.G could get to them too. The Renegades have helped our family stay under the radar and they have never done anything against us, but they are vulnerable too. Their leader is named Maximus Harris and he has a communication device that cannot be hacked into. He will attempt to get you this device if anything happens to me. Take it and use nothing other than this device to communicate electronically with anyone. Stay away from cell phones.

John, Maximus has suspicions about you and I'm not exactly sure why. He mentioned that you had a certain "gift" that could get you into a lot of trouble. I hope he wasn't referencing anything bad that you have done. Maximus told me that...

He has suspicions about me? He had to be referencing my visions. But how would he know that I had visions? I tried to think back and one memory stuck out sharply. I was twelve and I was about to go to sleep when suddenly I was dreaming that I was in that alleyway. There was a man in the alley that, looking back, he had to have been Maximus. I didn't know it then but this wasn't a dream, it was a vision.

I was remembering it clearly, like it was yesterday. The walls of the alleyway raced to the sky as I made my usual route home. My backpack was heavy and my forehead was beading with sweat. As soon as I realized where I was, I staggered, unable to stand upright. I dropped my backpack and looked around carefully at my surroundings. I definitely knew something freaky was going on. Above me was a blue sky like you would see in the middle of the day. There were no clouds and the sun was where it

204

would have been in the early afternoon. My mind was racing. *What was going on? How did I get here? Is this a lucid dream?*

I thought I was all alone in the alley but I felt the presence of another human being. Tired and confused, I searched around for evidence of another person. Above me were the same broken panes plastered on the same grey mucky wall. Two walls were nearly touching each other but not close enough to stop someone from hiding in there. Next to me were the same trash cans I've seen for years, piled with garbage that overflowed. The trash cans rested under some stairs that didn't reach the ground. It was a fire escape. I'd have to jump several feet to reach the bottom step, which was joined to the other grey steps with rusted brown handles made of long metal poles. One well-thrown rock could easily break one of the poles off its hinges, I thought. More stairs were placed along the same wall but higher than the first flight. Only an assassin like Aguilar could jump and reach those stairs. Two more flights of stairs followed the first two and they stopped at a door in the wall. It was really high but I could see the number 41 painted in a fading gold color on the door, and a dirty gold doorknob. At that time I never thought anyone actually lived in that place, but in light of this new information it must have been the base of the Renegades. The presence I felt grew. I turned around and in the empty space behind me was a man. The man wore a mask and some kind of uniform. He stared at me so I stared back at him. The man stood right in the middle of the alley, like he was in a play and was blocking the choreography. But was he going to say any lines? Silence continued so I said, "You know this isn't the 1900's. I have a cell phone and I can call the police."

"There will be no need for that," he said. "I am here to help you understand the world around you, John."

I froze, unable to comprehend how he knew my name. "Stalkers go to prison even if they hide behind a mask," I told him, trying to conceal the fact that I was shaking. I slowly moved closer to my backpack because my phone was in it.

"I am not a stalker, John, just hear me out."

"Don't call me, John. You don't know who I am!" Now my voice was obviously shaking.

"Okay, but you need to know what is going on before it's too late for you," he said, which terrified me.

"I already know what's going on!" I blurted out, thinking he was surely going to kill me. Then in one movement I grabbed my backpack, lifted it on top of my shoulders, and sprinted home as fast as I could away from that creepy place.

When I woke up in my bed sweating and panting, I knew something was sketchy--it was just too real. Later that day after school, I was walking home through that alley. The same trash cans, walls, and stairs, door, were all there. The sky was just like it was in my dream, blue and clear. I started to get scared and when I turned around there was a figure behind me just like the one in my dream. I immediately shouted, "I know what is going on in the world and don't call me John!" Before he could say anything, I was already running away.

So I did have visions in the past, but I was too clueless to notice that something absolutely insane was happening. Maximus must have had suspicions about me because of that encounter in the alleyway. He must have known that I knew somehow that he would be there. And I had suspicions about him because I must have recognized him, maybe his voice, when he was posing as a cashier at the gun store.

I tried hard to stop my mind from jumping from one question to another so I could read the rest of my mom's note.

...Maximus told me that the T.F.G. grows stronger every time more fourteen-year-olds get their shots. Listen carefully. The majority of the world is controlled by Crofar and is commanded to follow his orders. The catch is that Crofar could be putting some members on auto-pilot while manually controlling others. The ones controlled manually are the most dangerous because Crofar personally controls them with different settings electronically. Those people tend to be the T.F.G. soldiers and Crofar's personal bodyguards. What's different about the manually controlled is that Crofar allows them some of their own decision making power and they can kill you more easily. The shot that everyone gets when they turn fourteen gives a wireless connection to Crofar's computer which allows Crofar to control the mind of that person. Crofar is the Queen Ant. If you kill him, you kill his colony.

Do you see what I'm saying? They are limited! Without the T.F.G. army of controllers, there is no population of controlled! At least until they figure out how to make a serum that works on everyone, but they have been trying for years to do that, and as far as I know, they haven't figured it out yet.

But there is no time to waste! One of the things your father and I found while hacking into their database was that the T.F.G. is headquartered in Amber City and it's where all their plans are made and where everything is stored. This place was really hard to find. It is near the doctor's office we took you to when you were supposed to get your shot. If our mission failed at the shot clinic, you're going to need to gain access to this facility. If you are going to stop them, you must destroy it.

"Hey, watcha doing?" I whipped around to see Hazel looking at me sweetly with her blue eyes.

"Umm... nothing," I lied.

208

"Then what's that?" Hazel pointed towards the letter that was illuminating the screen.

"Oh, that is…those are…instructions," I told her while I unplugged the jump drive and closed the lid of the laptop. The jump drive was hot when I shoved it in my pocket.

"Oh, you finally took out the jump drive," Hazel said.

I threw my arms up in surrender and then brought them down to my shirtless sides. "You got me."

Hazel looked down at me and said, "Put on a shirt. I'll wait for you."

I got up and motioned to Hazel that I was watching her by using two fingers pointed at my eyes and then at hers. She tilted her head and gave me a smile so I headed towards my room. My room was almost as big of a mess as it was before, but the cleanup would have to wait. The rest of the letter would have to wait too. I picked up the wallet I left on the floor and squeezed the jump drive into it. I then grabbed one of my new shirts, threw it on and returned to the kitchen where Hazel was waiting for me politely.

"So what was on the jump drive?" Hazel asked. She wasn't going to give up.

"I told you. Instructions," I said, a little too defensively.

To my surprise, she did give up. She didn't say another word about it. She didn't question what the instructions were about or who wrote them. Hazel only stared me down, like she was willing me to blurt out more information all on my own. I almost did but then the corners of her mouth rose up in a smile. "I was thinking that we could possibly go out to get some real weapons today," she suggested. "The ones we have are lame and I don't think we can really protect ourselves if we need to. Besides, it's a great day for wearing my new jacket."

"Yeah," I replied, a little creeped out that Chase and Hazel were shaping the battle to come without any suggestions from me. "Chase had the same idea," I told her, "we were just waiting for you to get up. Do you want some breakfast before we go?"

"Yeah. I can get it myself," she said, asserting her independence.

"Don't worry, I got it," I said to her, motioning for her to sit down. "So what do you want to eat?"

"I know this is weird," she replied, "but I was going to eat some of that veggie tray in the fridge. I noticed you guys aren't exactly fighting over it."

She was right about that. I was thinking how glad I would be to see that thing gone as I piled a bunch of veggies on a big plate and stuck a bowl of ranch dressing in the middle and delivered it to the amazing Hazel. I couldn't believe how much I liked doing things for her. I would never have done this for Chase. I wasn't sure if this was love, but I really liked it. I wondered if I could call her my girlfriend. A girlfriend was never something I wanted but I was starting to see why other people did. The way she smiled or talked to me always made me feel happier and more uplifted. Could I be in love if I'm only in eighth grade? I wished I had my parents to talk to about this.

While Hazel munched on carrots and celery, which I did not understand at all, I headed to Chase's room to see what was up with him. I knocked on his door and Chase yelled at me to come in. Chase was trying on his new clothes and he was clearly not happy. "Dude, how do you live wearing this kind of stuff?" All I could do was laugh. He did look kind of ridiculous costumed in my taste. I never even thought about buying things that *he* would like. "Next time we go shopping," he said, "I'm going. You have the fashion sense of an old man!"

"You can always wear that same stinky junk you've had on for days," I told him as he rolled his eyes and pulled his new shirt down to stretch it out.

"Whatever," Chase said, "This will do for now. Are we going to the weapons store? I heard Hazel up. *Finally.*"

"Yeah, let's do it," I replied and then headed to my own room. I picked up the wallet and the jump drive fell out. I picked it up and held it for a second, thinking about my mom's words. I felt like I was holding this magical device, this conduit that went directly to my mom. "We are almost there, mom." I whispered. "We are almost there."

CHAPTER 19

"Let's go," I shouted from my room as I finished tying my shoes.

"Yup," I heard each of them say, already at the front door waiting for me.

"Okay! Who's excited to get some killer weapons?!" I asked, hurrying to the door to meet them with both of my hands in the air as if it were a dance party.

"I am!" Chase said sarcastically, jumping in excitement to mock me. Hazel wasn't that animated but she did show a happy sneer. I could tell she really did want to get some killer weapons.

"What about the security camera?" Hazel asked. "Shouldn't someone be here to watch?"

"Well, if someone robs our house," Chase replied, continuing his mocking tone, "I won't blame it on you."

"Jerks," Hazel said calmly, as she punched a fist into Chase's shoulder sending him off balance and prompting an little whimper.

"C'mon children, let's go," I said, gently shoving them through the doorway. It was already after noon and we were finally making our way out of our forest home and into the semi-populated streets. We were already too comfortable in this place, forgetting to be on the watch for anything unusual like Maximus had warned us to do. We acted like kids and talked the whole time about a variety of things. We discussed what to buy at the store. We discussed who had the best taste in clothes. I thought Hazel looked great in her new jacket and I made sure I said so. We discussed what someone would steal from our house if they did break in. Chase thought it would be the laptop and I said it would be the poptarts and we all laughed. We discussed pineapple topping on pizza. Hazel said that she liked this fruit on her pizza but Chase and I strenuously disagreed. With all the talking we did, it seemed like the walk to Amber Arms only took a few minutes.

But we never made it inside the store. "Get in the car!" I heard someone say as the three of us were pulled into the open door of a big van that barely waited for our feet to be off the ground before it was speeding away. "Are you *crazy*?" one of the men screamed, "that's the last place the three of you should be showing your faces! The T.F.G. is all over it in there! They are just waiting for you to do something stupid, like *buy guns*!"

It was Maximus, and as soon as he said it, I knew he was right. I was so fixated on changing the outcome of that first vision that I simply assumed we were going to have to buy the weapons that we used in the second vision, when Hazel wears her new jacket and kicks some T.F.G. butt with some serious firepower.

"Yeah, I guess after what happened last time we were here, it was pretty dumb to come back," Chase admitted, letting his head hang down in shame. Hazel looked embarrassed too.

"This is my fault, Maximus," I said, "I don't know what I was thinking."

"You weren't," Maximus snapped back. "Don't let that happen again."

"Where are we going?" Hazel wanted to know, looking through the only window in the van--the windshield.

"You need weapons? I'm going to make sure you have weapons. I have a feeling John knows where we are going. Am I right, John?" Maximus glared at me, daring me to spill the beans about my visions. I glared back.

"You mean you have a weapons stash in your apartment?" I asked.

"Ha!," Maximus replied, "That's not my apartment. That whole row of buildings in that alley is our base. The Renegades have been holed up in there for years, hiding from the T.F.G. and gathering intel. We've figured out a few things about how their serum works, and your mom and dad were a huge help. Still, as dumb as your little crew was today, you've gotten us closer to their base than we've ever been before. I'm guessing you've even seen the inside of it. Is that right, John?"

I glanced quickly at Hazel and then Chase and felt my mouth go completely dry. I was exposed and my two best friends were going to be pissed for not hearing this from me. "Yeah," I choked out, "something like that."

Chase reacted immediately. "I knew you were hiding something, dude. Not cool."

216

"Cool yourself, kid," Maximus said in my defense, "We've all got a big problem and it's time to work together."

"He's right. I should have told you earlier but I was trying to work out what was happening myself. I have these dreams, but they're more like visions. They are incomplete but I'm pretty sure they are visions of the very near future. Except that it can change. And because of that, I didn't want to complicate things by adding this news to our decisions about what to do." My confession felt good but neither of my friends were happy to hear it.

"Why the hell not?" Chase demanded. "What else aren't you telling us? Tell me! Is there some scenario where we actually *live* through this?"

I suddenly realized that I was right all along to keep this to myself. This information was definitely going to change the future. *Damnit Maximus! Did you have to bring this up?* "I'm sorry," was all I could think to say, "I really don't know." And that was the truth.

Suddenly the van stopped. I could see through the windshield that we were now in the dreaded alleyway. Even though it was early afternoon, it was very dark in there, like it always was. Then the ground in front of us opened up like a clam and our van was swallowed whole. We crept along a very tight passageway that was just big enough for this vehicle to barely get through. That descended into a cavern that was dimly lit. There were no windows anywhere and at first I didn't even notice that there were more people down there. A lot more people. Everyone was dressed in black and heavily armed.

"We're here," Maximus announced. "*Now* you can shop for weapons. Just don't take anything you don't know how to use."

Chase and Hazel were mesmerized by this spectacle. There were weapons lining one whole side of this massive space. Hazel and I walked toward the left and Chase wandered off to the right. There were guns, knives, grenades, and weapons I didn't even recognize. Everything was engraved with a circle emblem just like the weapons we used in my last vision. This was definitely where we get our new weapons, I thought. That was pretty freaky in itself. If we hadn't stupidly gone to Amber Arms, we would not have been picked up by Maximus, and we wouldn't be where we needed to be to get the weapons that we actually used in the vision. It was almost like that mistake was meant to be.

Hazel quietly looked at all the deadly weapons around her. She was drawn to the personal weapons, picking up guns and knives and weighing them in her hands, which seemed so delicate to me. But here she was seriously considering which of these killing machines was right for her. I didn't want to influence her decision so I said nothing while she continued her search. I spied bayonets stacking one shelf and I couldn't help testing their sharp tips with my finger. They were about one foot in length and I briefly thought that having a bayonet attached to our guns would be aesthetically pleasing; but bayonets were not in the vision and this was not the Civil War.

I glanced along the wall taking in the many different types of guns, knives, bayonets, carbines, grenades, rockets, torpedoes-- mostly everything we didn't need. I was surprised to see torpedoes. Chase was at the far end looking at flamethrowers. I left Hazel and walked over to him. He turned his head and scratched his chin like he was contemplating the usefulness of this weapon for our particular goals. "Pretty cool, right?" he asked, pointing to the X15 flamethrower directly in front of him. Footsteps interrupted our moment of devotion.

219

"Yeah, sorry guys but that one counts as one you don't know how to use," Maximus said pulling the beast off the shelf to show us how heavy it was, and cumbersome. It had two poles and a tube connecting it to a tank. "Besides, your mom would be pretty disappointed in me if she knew I was helping you *like this*," he added. He was trying to remind me that he was a friend of my mom's, but also an ally of mine. She was gone and now we had to defeat the T.F.G., maybe with tactics that she would never have approved.

"Fine," Chase said crossly, walking away. Maximus looked at me for a minute like he wanted to say something, but then he walked away too. I sighed and tried to clear my mind. Sometimes days started out badly but they changed. I had actually started out thinking that today was going to be fun. But that was such a kid way of thinking. And here we were looking at weapons like kids in a candy store. We wanted everything. Was I supposed to be like a parent or a supervisor over my friends?

Parents. Dammit. Why was I constantly being reminded of my parents? It felt like every single idea or thought that came to my head always led to my parents. And the fact that I am an orphan.

220

And the fact that one person, one leader, one man, can do all this. He took my parents, my home, my regular fourteen year old life. My parents are dead but I don't even know what that means except that I can't feel their life line. I can't feel their pulse of life. I don't even know why they existed, why they walked on this Earth with such hope just to lose it. They didn't need to bring me into this world too. I'm useless. I am holding on to my life and my friends and fighting this mind-controlling maniac but I don't even know why. What difference will it make? It won't bring my parents back. My life just seems like one shaky terrifying ride. But it isn't a ride, or a film. It's not even cells and matter struck together under stretchy skin. My life feels like a flimsy string held in place by weak tape from one side of a wall to the other in a windstorm. Air whips and twists the string every which way until it tugs the tape from the walls and lets it hit the floor in a tangled lump. And the wind just blows that around too, whispering mockingly, "You haven't seen it all." That is what life is. A human being beaten numerous times by something he can't control. A force unknown to him.

"John, over here!" Chase called. My gaze at the flamethrower faded as I looked over to see Chase and Hazel together across the room. They had a number of things on a table that they had pulled off their shelves. "We found some really cool guns! And knives!"

Maybe it was going to be a better day after all. "Alright! That's what I like to hear," I said, perking up. I headed over to their table of goods when Maximus yelled for Chase to come look at something. Chase literally ran to Maximus like a puppy going for a treat. I figured Maximus was going to show Chase something very cool that was a little less ridiculous than a flamethrower. I seized the moment to talk to Hazel. "Hazel," I said, diverting her attention away from the stash that she wanted me to see. But as soon as her eyes were on me, I paused, stumbling to find the right words.

"What is it, John?"

"I just...I just..."

Hazel smirked and pivoted toward me like she was going to wait all day for me to find the right words. "You just *what?*"

But words were still jumbled in my mouth. It was as if I was playing Scrabble with my family. "Economics," my mom would say followed by a hair flick as she dropped the "C' on a double letter score and the rest over a triple word score attached to a dangling 'E'. "Let's see," she would say and then slowly add up all her points so we could verify that she was crushing us. "That's 18 times 3, which is 54, plus 50. That's 104 points. Not bad." Mom was always proud of her work. Meanwhile I'd be sitting there with my second grade vocabulary trying to figure out where to put my 'Z' and four 'I's.

That's how I felt right then too, but I just had to throw something on the board no matter how minor it would be. It was my turn: "I just wanted to say I'm sorry for not telling you about my visions. And there's something else I didn't tell you. Earlier when I was looking at the laptop? I was reading a note from my mom."

She shifted her weight and uncrossed her arms. Her expression completely changed. "Wow, John, now I feel like a complete idiot when I acted all happy and flirty when you just read something that was probably very hard to read." Hazel then

223

took hold of my hands. "I like you a lot John, so please tell me the truth and I'll do my best to understand."

"I will," I replied, feeling sad that I had made her feel foolish.

"John, do you promise? I have to be able to trust you." Hazel looked at me with those sweet puppy eyes. I squeezed her warm hands gently and leaned in to whisper into her ear.

"I promise," I said, and then kissed her lightly on the cheek.

Footsteps broke into our moment. Chase and Maximus approached carrying a large box. I figured it was ammo and I was partly right. Hazel quickly cleared a space and they dropped it into the spot. "Alright," Maximus began, opening the top of the box. "We have some things to discuss." Maximus pulled out a folded map and spread it out over the weapons on the table. It laid there unevenly and awkwardly creased but he didn't seem to care. I could immediately see that it was a map of Amber City, much like the one we had found in the cupboards of our rental house, but bigger. "Chase has informed me that the T.F.G. base is *under* this area right here," he said, pointing to an area on the map that Chase had circled. "That's an impressive bit of detective work."

Chase was beaming. His genius was finally being acknowledged. "He also mentioned that the three of you have a plan to get into this base and….and….and...*do what?*"

Chase's smile faded quickly but Maximus was looking at me. I started thinking about my vision, and then what my mom told me in the letter on the jump drive. "Well," I said, "every T.F.G. soldier controls *someone*. So the more soldiers we take out with our weapons, the more people we free."

"So your plan is to kill as many T.F.G. soldiers as you can?" Maximus asked. "And if you don't kill them all? Or is your plan to kill them all?"

Chase and Hazel looked at me and then down at the floor. My gut was churning and I felt like I was going to pass out. We really had nothing. How could three teenagers take out the entire T.F.G. army? I fell back against the table and used it to prop myself up. No one spoke for what seemed like a long time.

"Right," Maximus continued. "I'm glad we had this conversation."

225

"Wait," I blurted out, remembering what my mom said about their pyramid scheme. "If we take out the leader of the T.F.G., then the whole scheme falls, right? That's all we have to do. Take out Crofar. He's in that base, so we get in there, find Crofar, and kill Crofar. He's the reason my parents are dead! He's the reason we are fighting for our lives! We have to kill Crofar!"

Maximus stepped back and let his head fall forward. He took a deep breath and sighed. He spoke quietly, almost like he was talking just to himself. "I suppose that *is* what we have to do, but I'm not sure you actually have a plan for doing that. The T.F.G. is heavily armed. Even if you get in there and make it to Crofar without getting killed by his army, I'm not sure you will be able to take him out. He's a tricky bastard. Look at what he pulled off in Amber Arms the last time we thought we had him."

"What other choice do we have?" Hazel interjected. "Sooner or later, they are going to find us and then we'll be nothing but three more teenagers who can't think for themselves."

"Well, we certainly don't want that," Maximus replied, "but if a suicide mission is your plan A, I'd advise against it. Look, all I'm saying is go home with your new weapons and keep

226

yourselves safe. When it's time to go on the offense, I will let you know. Got it? Now let's get this stuff together and get you back home."

CHAPTER 20

It was late afternoon and the streets were eerily quiet. So was the inside of the van. When we pulled up to the house, we hurried in with the box that we took from the Renegade's base. It was so heavy that it took two of us to carry it in. We locked the door behind us as the van sped away.

Chase sat down at the laptop and watched our front porch as the sun was hovering just above the top of the trees. "This is ridiculous," he said. "What, are we just going to wait for them to come to us? And if Maximus is so concerned about our plan, I didn't hear him come up with a better one. Hazel is right, we have no choice but to sneak into their base and try to do *something!*"

"I agree!" Hazel said, looking up from the box of weapons and ammo she had been rummaging through. "Screw Maximus and his Renegade cowards!"

"I say we go tonight," Chase added, feeding off of Hazel's enthusiasm. "C'mon, John, what do we have to lose?"

"We only have pistols and knives but I think that's all we need," Hazel added, laying out our arsenal on the floor. Chase and I surveyed the deadly pieces of aluminum alloy. She was right about one thing; we didn't need nuclear weapons. We just need something we could handle that could kill the soldiers I had seen in my dreams.

"Well," Chase beckoned, "What say you, fearless leader?"

I was seriously conflicted. My visions told me that our mission basically fails. That the Renegades have to come save us. On the other hand, these visions only seem to show me what happens if x, where x is a variable that can change in the present. I proved that by talking Hazel into getting a different jacket. Maybe things in the future have changed now that Chase and Hazel know about my visions. "Alright," I relented, "on one condition."

"Yeah, what's that?" Chase played along.

I made a simple request: "We leave in the morning, right before dawn at the earliest. I want one more chance to dream about this mission. Deal?"

"Deal!" my friends said in unison.

Chase immediately grabbed a black boot knife from the spread on the floor. It was definitely a long knife--bigger than Chase's head. I became anxious to get a knife too so I went into the pile and grabbed a kukri knife. It had a brown wood-like handle and a silver blade that curved and tapered into a super-sharp point. This is definitely what I need, I thought. Hazel picked up a gun and pointed it at the laptop, pretending to fire. "Can't wait to start using this monster," she said smiling.

We spent another hour loading guns and outfitting ourselves. Soon my stomach was making noises and I retreated to the kitchen to see what we had left to eat. There was an unopened box of miniature cheeseburgers in the freezer and that was about it. I popped the whole box in the microwave and when the timer went off I stuffed one whole steaming burger into my mouth and placed the rest on a single plate to share. When it went down my throat I could feel my digestive system pulling and breaking the food into smaller pieces.

"So let's discuss the plan for tomorrow's mission," I said, setting the plate of burgers on the table next to the laptop, which drew both of their attention immediately.

Chase swallowed a whole cheeseburger as fast as he could and then said, "Ok, so we will bring our weapons and my map." He laid out his map and pointed to a spot on its surface not far from our house. "Here is the entrance of the base."

"Then what?" Hazel asked, grabbing two cheeseburgers before they were devoured by Chase and me.

"We should cut the power so we can stealthily move about the base," Chase responded. "I can do that. Their power source is here," he added, pointing to another spot on the map. Then he shot up and went over to the big box of ammo. After a quick scan, he smiled and pulled out some bolt cutters and headlamps. We were so focused on weapons that we didn't think about all the other things we might need. "Thank you, Maximus!"

We each grabbed a headlamp and put it on. This worried me, but also made me hopeful. My previous visions were full of flashing lights and I don't remember any of us wearing a headlamp. "We have two main objectives," I said, "we need to find and kill Crofar--that's number one. Anyone that gets in our way has to be taken out too. So we need to bring plenty of ammunition."

"And our second objective?" asked Hazel.

"Well, if this doesn't work. I mean, if we can't get to Crofar, we need to at least destroy their stock of serum. Or the procedure to make it. Or both. Hell, we may need to destroy the whole base. I don't think we have what we need to do that, so our second objective is to learn as much as we can about this base, just in case we ever get another chance to defeat the T.F.G. We need information."

"I'll take the killing part," Hazel declared while chewing her food.

"We are so close," Chase observed, "I can almost taste victory. We will finally be able to live normally."

"Are you sure you want that?," I asked. "Are you sure you want to go back to living a life with loud rude people all around you telling you what to do and say? I mean come on, look around, it's so peaceful."

Chase scrunched his eyebrows and glared at me with an expression of utter disbelief. "Yeah, it's peaceful, but this peace is the wrong kind of peace. The T.F.G. is controlling people's *minds* and that is *wrong*. Imagine if we had gotten that shot. We would have lost our freedom. Our lives would no longer be ours. Would you really lose the only real experience life has given you to win *silence?*"

That's all I wanted to hear. Chase was one hundred percent in. I could feel his great passion for justice and passion can get you anywhere. "You're right. Thanks for reminding me how terrible this society is. I needed a reminder."

Our burgers were gone and I started thinking that it wouldn't be that easy to get into their base, cut the power, and stealthily kill their leader. Was it even possible? Was Maximus right that this was a suicide mission? "Okay guys," I said, clearing the one plate that we all ate off of. "I'm going to bed. Set your alarms for 4:00 a.m."

"Sweet dreams, John," Chase quipped. "And I've never been more sincere about *that.*"

"Yeah," Hazel added, "If it's more like a nightmare, feel free to sleep in." That was enough to get both me and Chase laughing, though in an uneasy way, and on that note I left them for my room.

That's when things started to get weird. I got into my bed and tried to fall asleep, but like usual, I couldn't go to sleep. I must have been lying there for a good ten minutes with my eyes closed concentrating on willing myself to sleep, which never worked. When I opened my eyes I could see a light outside my window and wondered if it had been there before. I hadn't noticed it before so I got up and went over to the window. I moved the curtain to get a better look but the light then disappeared. Was something going on out there? Surely Chase would notice if someone was out there. But I had a bad feeling and decided to go check the laptop.

I expected to find Chase sitting there watching our porch through the laptop, but even though the lights were still on in the house, Chase wasn't there and the laptop was gone too. "Chase," I called out looking toward his room, first at a regular volume and then louder, "*CHASE?*" I got no response and when I looked in

234

his room, he wasn't there either. I considered the possibility that he was outside with his headlamp--maybe it was Chase I saw from my window. So I went to Hazel's room and knocked on her door. "Hazel," I called from the hallway, "Are you awake? I can't find Chase."

Nothing. I was starting to feel queasy. I was really getting scared. I opened Hazel's door and she was not in her room. At this point, I could not breathe. *Okay*, I thought, desperate to calm myself down, *maybe they are both outside. I don't know why, but there's no need to panic.* I felt like I had no choice but to check outside, but as soon as I cracked open the front door, I knew something was very wrong. Not that I could do anything about it. With my hand still on the door knob, it was tugged wide open from the outside and I was thrust into a masked figure holding a stun-gun meant for me.

CHAPTER 21

This time my dream was not about the future--it was about the past. I was sitting at a table with Chase. My waxy paper cup was filled to the brim with a sweet soda mix I liked to call Spriterade. Chase and I invented this name when we were thinking of what to call a mix between Powerade and Sprite. But for this drink to be called Spriterade, we decided, you need to have the Blue Mountain Berry blast Powerade. Once when Chase and I were in a Tiger Express, we saw a kid get Sprite and the green Powerade called Black Cherry Lime so we told him off because any drink that's green is just bloody disgusting. And *that* is what I was dreaming about.

"Come on," Chase was saying to that kid, "have you ever seen a kid with Gatorade options of blue, red, orange, purple, or green choose the green flavor? With all of those amazing other flavors why would you choose the green, sour apple flavor, when you could have chosen a refreshing red berry flavor? That doesn't make any sense."

Then the dream morphed into Hazel adding sugar and lemon juice to her iced tea. She looked at me the whole time she was stirring her drink, and then she took the straw to her lips and winked at me. "Really?" Chase said, ruining the moment, "who drinks tea when you could get a can of soda? Tea is terrible. Juice with pulp is horrible. Lemonade is sickeningly sour. Why can't everybody just drink soda?"

Then Hazel started to cry. "I never went to a formal school," she declared out of nowhere. "My mom home-schooled me my whole life and I really miss her. Every time I think about her, it just makes me cry. I'm not used to crying like this. I feel like a kid whose balloon has popped. I have no control over anything."

"Gosh this is so freaking scary," Chase said, again completely disconnected from Hazel's emotional disclosure. "Did you ever think that three teenagers would have a chance to save the world?"

It was like I was watching a nonsensical movie. I couldn't speak or participate or turn it off. The last thing I heard was Chase telling me to get on a moving roller-coaster and as I jumped on, I instantly felt myself rushing forward and then flying off the rails. Just before I hit the ground, my body jerked me awake from my senseless vision, and I knew exactly where I was: cuffed to a metal gurney, being pushed down a brightly lit hallway by four T.F.G. soldiers. Just like my first vision, but now it's not a vision anymore, it is reality.

"Where are my friends?" I demanded.

"Shut up, kid!" I heard right before one of them punched me in the face and I was out. Except I wasn't all the way out. The soldiers wheeled me into a large brightly lit room. The white walls reflected so much light that I squinted just to make out the face looming over me. It was Crofar.

With a big grin on his long face, he spoke harshly to the soldiers that had escorted me in, "Get out! I will summon you when I need you to return."

When I heard the door slam shut behind me, I said, weakly, "Where are my friends?" as if I had the right to demand answers in my current predicament. That really made him laugh.

"You think you're something, John. Well, I suspect you don't even know how right you are," he said, turning around to the large white table behind him. As he reached across the table for a single key, I could see that he was unarmed. The next thing I knew, he was releasing my restraints, starting with my feet. "Before you think you're going to jump up off that gurney and beat me to death with your bare fists," he said, grinning, "you should bear in mind that I have injected you with serum which is why the room looks like a blurry sun. Also, in my left hand I have one of my favorite things, a button. As soon as I press it, ten guards come through that door and fill you with bullets. Got it?"

I looked around me to see where I was but I couldn't tell due to whatever Crofar injected me with. But I did realize that I had to be in the T.F.G. base because this moment was reenacting what I saw in my first vision except the guards didn't hurt me, I wasn't drunk, and Crofar showed up to brighten my day. Did something I do change the future which is now my present?

239

"What do you want with me?" I demanded. "Why not just give me that shot and get it over with? Take control of my mind, like you did with everyone else? Is that what you've done with my friends? Where are they?"

"*Friends?*" he said, dragging out the word. "Do you really think they are your friends? I wouldn't be so sure, John. When my soldiers infiltrated your little hideout, those two ran like terrified mice into the forest, leaving you all alone to be abducted. I doubt you'll ever see them again, and not because we have anything to do with it. They are cowards, John, and they have abandoned you."

I wasn't sure what to think but the idea of them running away stung like a punch to my gut. Crofar was probably lying and I certainly had no reason to trust him. "Good!" I said as convincingly as I could, "I'm glad they escaped! That was always our plan."

Crofar stared at me and then his mouth slowly curled into that big grin again. He finished removing the shackles from my hands. "You really don't know why you're here, do you?"

I sat up slowly and looked down at my red wrists, rubbing them. My whole body was in pain. He must know I have visions, I thought. But taken from my house to meet with the leader of the T.F.G. didn't make any sense. *Why didn't he just have the soldiers give me that shot?*

"I'm going to let you in on a little secret, John. Your parents had been a thorn in my side for a long time, way before they decided to destroy one of my shot clinics. I guess they told you a thing or two about our little organization. That's all they could have told you--a thing or two--they never got very much as far as intel goes."

Crofar couldn't talk without laughing. It was infuriating, especially since he was talking about my parents who were both dead because of him. "But they did have something they didn't even know they had," he snickered, "they were immune to my serum! They were immune! The whole damn family is immune, John! You've had your shots! You've had your shots and you are immune!"

His snickering escalated into a crazy grinning gasping as he spoke. I thought he was going to hyperventilate. I couldn't get my head around what was he telling me. "So I'm going to make you an offer you can't refuse, John," he said, finally winding down. "If you want to live, you'll work for me. If you don't want to work for me, you won't live. Is that clear enough for you?"

"What am I supposed to do for you?" I asked, trying to buy time. "I'm just a kid!"

"I'm glad you asked, John." I was getting tired of hearing my name every time he said something. "I want to know where the Renegades are hiding," he finished.

He knew about the Renegades, and that I knew about the Renegades. My hands started to shake and I brought them up across my chest like I was cold. I was cold. Crofar laughed and threw a jacket at me, which I quickly put on. The jacket bore the T.F.G. insignia--I already looked like I was working for him. "Suppose I know what you're talking about, which I don't," I replied, "what guarantee do I have that you won't kill me as soon as I've given you what you want, which I will never do?"

Crofar's face contorted into the evilest grin I had seen yet. "What choice do you have," he shook with laughter, "but to trust me?" Then he lifted up his left hand and showed me a small device with a black button tucked into his closed fist. And then the whole world went into slow motion as I watched his thumb make contact and then press it down.

An explosion of gunfire sent me straight to the ground where I covered my head, closed my eyes, and waited to be killed. I heard crashing and banging, like the whole room was collapsing. I wondered how all this mayhem could be precise enough not to kill Crofar too. Maybe we were both going down. That would be some small comfort, I thought. But just as suddenly as it started, the noise stopped. I didn't move for a long time--I don't know how long--but when the quiet seemed to hold, I opened my eyes and lifted my head. I could finally see where I was, the long bright hallway from my first vision. Crofar wasn't there anymore. Was this another damn hologram?

What happened from here forward was the same order of events that I saw in my earlier visions. My friends found me and since I was still recovering from that drug Crofar put in me, they asked me if I was brainwashed which I replied weakly, "No." Crofar was lying--my friends had not abandoned me. We kept running until we reached a familiar office with two newspapers that I shoved in my pocket.

"Maximus? Thank god it's you," I heard Hazel say from outside the office.

"Dude, it's the Renegades!!!" This time the voice came from someone next to me. I turned to see Chase as wave of relief spread through my core. But the good feeling was short-lived when I comprehended what would happen next. Right as the realization entered my mind, the next event I knew by heart occurred.

In front of me was a rectangle of light. But the light in front of me was just a reflection from the light behind me. In a second the reflected light stopped and everything went black. I was blind. There was darkness all around me. The only thing sensible was sound. "Yeah, we've got to get out of here," I could hear Maximus say in the darkness, "where are your friends?"

Then in an instant the lights came on again, illuminating the room so that I could see Maximus and the Renegades huddled around Hazel. But then I couldn't see them again. The source of the light was above Hazel and it had just gone out again. "John and Chase are inside that room," Hazel said, gesturing toward us as the light went back on. Then Maximus said some things that I didn't recall occurring in my visions. "Thank god. You're a life saver Hazel, this rescue mission might actually succeed!" The Renegades all turned and looked straight at us.

"Well what are you waiting for?" Maximus yelled, "Let's go!"

Chase and I sprinted out of the room to regroup with our allies. We knew the lights would be off again soon enough, and we were right.

"Everybody get in a single file line and grab onto the person in front of you," Maximus commanded in the darkness.

I grabbed onto Chase and a soldier grabbed onto me. The light came back on and the line lunged forward. I was impressed with this strategy, thinking there was no question why Maximus was the leader of the Renegades. Chase moved forward pulling me with him. As long as there was light, we moved forward, fast. When the lights went out, we lurched back to a slow shuffle. Only Maximus at the front could see where we were going--the rest of us just had to trust him. Chase and I were in the middle of the line. I couldn't tell how many Renegades were in the line, or where exactly Hazel was, which made me nervous.

As we progressed it was obvious that the base had been abandoned. Not a single T.F.G. member was in sight. We passed office after office occupied only by furniture and paper. I felt the urge to break out of line and find out why no one was here to protect their base. Something seemed very wrong about this line of people--enemies of the T.F.G.--just walking down the hall heading for the door. Every step made me more nervous. Surely they were going to do *something* to stop us.

"Halt!" I heard someone yell from far in front of me. Chase came to a quick stop causing me and everyone behind me to bump into the person ahead. "Stay in the line," the same voice called out. I raised to the top of my toes to try to steal a glance of what was happening. Chase moved a bit to help me see but I wasn't tall enough.

Then a wave of low voices rose up in the hallway, getting louder and louder as it made its way through the line and back toward us. "They're going to knock down the door," was finally audible.

246

"Cool beans," Chase said, breaking the flow of information heading to the back of the line.

As I craned my head around the line of bodies ahead of me, I noticed a cloud of dust as the door blew open with a bang. "Let's move," Maximus yelled as our entire army went out without a hitch into the dark, cold night.

CHAPTER 22

"We're safe!" Chase exclaimed, like he couldn't believe it. I really didn't believe it. It was way too easy to get out of there. Where was everyone? What were they planning? What were we supposed to do now?

Maximus must have been thinking the same thing. "It's not safe for you kids to go home," he said. "You'll have to come back to our base tonight, at least until we figure out what our next move is." He glanced at me and did a double-take. "What the hell are you wearing, John?"

The jacket. He was asking about my official T.F.G. jacket. "Oh," I started, only to be cut off by Maximus.

"Save it for later," Maximus said, holding up his hand and looking past me. "We'll talk when it's safe to talk. And right now, it is not safe to talk."

I followed his eyes behind me where the blown door was laying on the ground. The lights inside the base were no longer going on and off and a rumbling coming from inside was getting louder. They were still in there and we had to get far away, and fast. Maximus gave some kind of arm signal and the Renegades scattered. Small groups ran off in every direction. "Follow me," Maximus said to me, Hazel, and Chase, as he sprinted in the direction of our house.

Maximus was fast and it was hard for Chase to keep up. We zigzagged a few times through the streets before I noticed a van parked by one of the houses. It looked like the same van that picked us up before when we were about to get ourselves killed at Amber Arms. As soon as we got close enough, the doors opened and again we were literally plucked from the street and pulled inside in a split second. The driver hit the gas the instant our feet were off the ground. The door wasn't even closed as we sped away.

Chase was huffing and puffing, trying to catch his breath, but Hazel was quiet and alert. Maximus was up front talking to the driver. "What happened to you guys," I asked, looking at Chase, "back at the house? I got up and you two were gone."

"It's very complicated," Chase said. "I'll let Hazel explain."

Hazel sighed annoyingly but did fill me in on the events. "The Renegades took Chase and me out to train and brainstorm future plans. They didn't take you because they wanted you to keep visioning. Chase and I came up with ideas for Maximus until we were about to pass out because of how tired we were, so Max drove us back home. Right as we got home, we noticed the security camera had fallen over. As worried and tired as we were, we checked the footage on the laptop and saw you get knocked out and taken to the T.F.G. base. Maximus then called his army on a rescue mission- to rescue you."

I must have been staring at her, dumbfounded by this revelation. The wheels in my head kept turning as I tried to comprehend her story. Hazel continued, "I think there's a lot more going on with the T.F.G. than we originally thought. They are smarter than we expected. The rescue mission is now in our past, so let's focus on what our next move is."

Maximus caught Hazel's words and turned back to face us from the front of the van. "Hazel is right, there is much more going on in there than we knew," he said. "My crew managed to pick up some intel in the base before we got the distress signal which told us your location and that you were safe."

"Distress signal?" I asked, remembering the device Maximus had given us but not remembering having it with me when I needed it.

"That was me," Chase chimed in. "We took it with us to the base as a signal."

"That was brilliant, man. Thanks!" I told Chase as he smiled proudly.

Maximus added to Chase's pride with a compliment of his own. "Chase also had the presence of mind to transmit all the intel he had compiled on the T.F.G. base from his laptop just before they went to find you." Then he added with a smirk, "I thought it was pretty stupid for your friends to go there without backup but I guess it worked out okay."

"I think I missed something," Chase said, looking serious for a change, "why does everyone think there's more to the T.F.G. than brainwashing everyone? Isn't that enough?"

"Yeah," replied Maximus, "that is bad enough. But it's worse. We've got to get to Crofar to stop this madness but he's got some super-holographic capability so he can be in two places at once, sort of. I mean, he can make a version of himself that is so lifelike you can't even tell you're standing there talking to no one."

"Right," Hazel remembered, "like that time you shot Crofar in the gun store but he wasn't really there."

"Exactly!" Maximus exclaimed, looking excited. My thoughts all connected now. When Crofar was talking to me, he actually wasn't there which is why he disappeared all of the sudden. "But here's the good news. My crew stole the jewels! I mean, the Renegades are now in possession of tech that makes those super-lifelike holograms possible! Crofar has the ability to make another version of himself, but he was trying to create that ability for all of his minions. Now we have that ability. They are testing the equipment even as we speak. As soon as we are sure we don't have a tail, we'll return to our base and regroup. I'm not sure how, but I have a feeling this might be very useful in our quest to stop the T.F.G."

"It might be too late," I said, bringing down the mood. Everyone stared at me waiting for me to finish the thought. "I picked up some papers off a desk in there. Not surprisingly, we are on Amber's Most Wanted list. But I just looked at the other one and I wish I would have done that sooner. Here's what it says." I produced the papers that were in my pocket and started reading: "Big Events Weekly. Gas Release. Beginning June 8, 2055, at 1:00 p.m., we will be releasing gas in the center of Amber. This gas is harmless and odorless and will replace the vaccine shots currently being administered to all children through the age of fourteen. This gas is a leap forward because it eliminates the need for shots and is safe for all ages. Thanks to this new invention, this gas will keep you healthy and clean from the moment you are born. Once we release the gas, it will spread throughout the city and vaccinate everyone. Using gas is better than ever, so please join us in Amber city as we release the future."

"What the…?" Chase said after I read it. "We are so friggin screwed. That's tomorrow."

Hazel looked like she had just come out of a horror movie. "I'm sure there is a way to stop the gas," Hazel said hopefully.

"You know, you're right," I said. "The T.F.G. gave us the exact location and time they are releasing the gas so if we appear at the place early, we can stop them."

"That's a great idea, John," Hazel said with a proud smile on her face.

"Good thinking! That might actually work," Chase said punching my shoulder.

Maximus grabbed the papers, read them quickly and then looked away for a minute. Finally he spoke. "I think it's a trap. If they put this in a newspaper, they want us to know. And they know we are going to try to stop them from releasing the gas. They are luring us to this location. I'm guessing there is no gas at all. Yet."

"Well, what if we get there early and surprise them?" Chase asked.

"I'm pretty sure that's what they expect," Maximus offered.

"But maybe there's a way to do what they expect, to be there, but not really be there," I suggested, looking at Maximus to see if he was thinking the same thing.

"Yes!" he said, "I'm right there with you! There's hardly enough time but if there is, it might just work!"

"Can someone fill me in?" Chase looked like he was trying to solve a riddle in a foreign language.

"Holograms!" Hazel practically shouted, "That's how we put ourselves in one place so we can be in another at the same time!"

"Bingo," Maximus said as his eyes flickered with excitement. "The only problem is that we kind of need to know what they are going to do so we can position ourselves." Maximus tightened as he processed that this plan was going to take longer than he expected. He looked at me very seriously and then laid on the pressure. "John, we need some future intel in a hurry. Do you have it in you?"

"How is this plan going to work if we don't know what to record until hours before they release the gas?" Chase asked.

"The T.F.G. isn't releasing a new invention, Chase. It's just a trap," Maximus stressed.

As I contemplated what Maximus was asking me to do, we rounded a corner I recognized and our van was swallowed whole by the street. Inside the Renegades' base we were quickly moved away from the main area and taken to a small studio apartment with a single steel door and no windows. It was sparsely furnished with bunk beds and there was a bathroom in the corner. There was no kitchen which I noticed right away because I was so hungry.

"You can sleep here," Maximus said to the three of us. "Give me a few minutes and I'll have some things brought over. Food, clothes, toothbrushes. Anything else?"

"When you say, "food," you don't mean a can of beans or something like that, do you?" Chase asked as he rubbed his belly. "I'm thinking we'll need a pizza. If you have it."

Maximus smiled and lifted one eyebrow. "I'll see what I can do about that," he said, and left us alone.

CHAPTER 23

Chase went over to the beds and tested each one. I walked over to an old couch on the opposite wall and sat down, hoping that Maximus would come back with a huge pepperoni pizza. Hazel sat down next to me and put her hand on top of mine.

"I'm really worried about tomorrow," Hazel said, as she moved her hand softly over my skin. I immediately stopped thinking about pizza.

"Why?" I asked, looking down at our hands, wishing this moment would never end.

"I don't know," she replied. "I just don't feel good about it. Promise me that we will make it through this. I want the chance to have a real relationship."

Before I could reassure her, there was a knock on the door and two guys came in with a couple boxes of stuff. Maximus was right behind them with a single plate covered with tinfoil.

Chase was the first there with his arms outstretched to relieve Maximus of his burden. As Chase peeled the foil back, his face fell. I could tell he was disappointed that it was not a pizza. But then he grabbed a little token off the plate and gobbled it up, burning his mouth in the process.

"C'mon guys. Pizza rolls!" Chase said, regaining his smile.

Hazel winked at me and pulled me up by my hand. In less than ten seconds we were scarfing down pizza rolls like there was no tomorrow. Maximus stood there for a minute watching us, like he was observing animals at the zoo tearing into raw meat. Finally, he shook his head, took the empty plate out of Chase's hand, and headed out the door. "Sweet dreams," he said, pulling the door closed behind him.

Chase plopped onto one of the top bunks and promptly fell asleep. Hazel and I curled up together in one of the bottom bunks, as far away from Chase as we could be. She put her head on my chest and I pulled the blanket over us. When I turned the light out I could feel her breathing change. I was caught between wanting to stay awake, stroking her hair, thinking about what we would do once this was all over; and going to sleep to find out what I could about tomorrow's confrontation with the enemy. But I was too tired for daydreaming about better days. I closed my eyes, combed my hand through Hazel's hair, and went to sleep.

I woke up in the middle of the city. Maximus, Hazel, and Chase stood by my side against an eight foot high wall that curved into a half circle around a raised concrete platform. From our vantage point, I could see out to a large grassy park with a pond in the distance. Straight ahead was a clocktower where a banner had been fixed: "Welcome to Amber, the most peaceful city in the world!" We were tucked into that semicircle as Crofar walked up the steps toward us, his evil grin spreading slowly across his face as he got closer. Behind him were about twenty soldiers, and we were unarmed. Crofar stopped about fifteen feet from us and started to laugh. "I see you have fallen into my trap. But only with your few, puny friends? Or are you expecting the Renegades to save you again? Yes, of course you are. You didn't have to lead me to the Renegades after all. I just had you bring them to me. You're a disappointment, John. I thought you were smarter than this." Crofar dropped his grin momentarily and glared at us with a disgusted look before he started to laugh again. "Even though you

you can have everything for yourself. You can kill us too but you'll never kill off the resistance. I'll make you a deal! Give this up or die! I promise you, whatever happens here, you will be defeated!"

Crofar laughed and said, "How cute. I'll take that as everybody's life then." He then shot each of my friends in the head and I watched them slump down onto the concrete one by one. Then he aimed his gun at my head and pulled the trigger.

I woke up with a gasp and sat straight up. My shirt was soaked with sweat and so was every other piece of clothing that was touching my body. I peeled the covers back and tried to roll out of bed quietly but I woke Hazel up.

"What did you dream?" She immediately asked. Her face was soft and her hair was a little wild. For that second looking at her I was happy.

"Something not good," I responded, returning my thoughts to the dream.

"Want to talk about it?" Hazel offered.

"No thanks. I have to process what happened first," I responded. I went to the bathroom and hoped Hazel would go back to sleep. Since there were no windows, I had no idea what time it was. I had to find Maximus and tell him what I saw. If we go to the center of the city to confront Crofar, we will be killed. I knew the only way we would stay alive was to break all the rules, which is exactly was Maximus was planning to do.

I left the room we were in and was startled to find so much activity taking place on the other side of the door. The Renegades were prepping for a showdown. I scanned the cavern where all of this was happening and saw Maximus far on the other side of it. He spotted me at the same time and walked toward me briskly, like a general in command of an army. Maximus was powerful and could make you feel like you were powerful too, but he was also a fatherly figure that had taken a liking to me and my friends. He opened the conversation with, "Hey John, how did you sleep?"

"It was good," I replied sarcastically. "I die today and so do you."

"What happened in your vision?" Maximus said, looking for details.

"Somehow you, Chase, Hazel and me end up facing off with him without weapons or backup and Crofar with an army at his back for protection shoots every single one of us in the head."

"John, you need to remember every single detail of this vision. Can you do that? Right down to the second. Where we are, what we say, what we do, what time it is when this happens. Do you have all of that information?"

"Crap! That's a lot of pressure," I blurted out as I tried to replay it all in my mind. The thing that was missing was the time. What time was it when we faced our executioner? I closed my eyes and tried to recall the clocktower that loomed over Crofar's head as he ascended the steps and moved into position. Suddenly it came into focus, like I was staring right at it. I was expecting it to be right around 1pm like the newspaper article said, but it wasn't. I expressed my surprise out loud. "It was 10:49 a.m!"

"Holy shit!" Maximus responded, "We don't have much time. Get your crew up and out here immediately. We've got work to do!"

Within ten minutes, the three of us were dressed and reporting for duty. Maximus looked us over and then faced me. "If you tell each of us exactly what we did in the vision you had last night, we will record ourselves on holograms and place them where they need to be. By the time he shoots us and the holograms disappear, my people will have stealthily attacked him from behind."

"I'm sorry, did you say Crofar *shoots* us?" Chase was his usual smart-ass self, which the rest of us had come to either appreciate or ignore, depending on the circumstances.

Maximus ignored Chase and focused on me again. "John, are we wearing what we should be wearing?" The shocking thing to me was that the stuff Maximus brought to us last night in the boxes, which we didn't even look at until this morning, was exactly what we were wearing in the vision I had last night. I gave Maximus a nod and he motioned one of his soldiers over to us. "Take them to the camera-room and I'll be there in a minute," he ordered, and then hurried off toward a gathering of soldiers near the weapons stockpile along the back wall.

The camera room was about the size of our bunk room but there were no bunks. There was a bathroom in the same corner but the room contained no furnishings at all. One wall had been painted black and there was a bunch of equipment in the middle of the room, including a large light table that was already softly illuminating the room. The set-up was pretty impressive and

Chase was checking it out. Hazel scrutinized the equipment like she was going to have to write a report. We waited in that state quietly for Maximus and I used the time to remember the vision again exactly as it went down.

I was the only one in the vision who said anything so telling Hazel, Chase, and Maximus what to do when we recorded them on a hologram wouldn't be a big deal. The most important thing was for me to talk at exactly the right time. If my hologram interrupted Crofar when he is talking, our plan will be revealed. So I needed to make sure I got everything exactly correct. I tried to convince myself that this was possible. I just needed to have a conversation with Crofar and fake getting shot in the head. This day was going to be suspenseful I could already tell. But if our holograms do everything as planned, we will attack from behind. Since Crofar has an army we will bring Maximus's army to match them. I wanted to take Crofar on one on one though.

Maximus opened the door and his tech person followed him in. She was tall with jet black hair and she wore everything black. She sat down in front of a computer without smiling or looking at us or saying anything. Maximus surveyed the room and walked over to the light table, motioning us over with his hand. On the table was a map of the city center. I could see all the landmarks that I had seen last night in my vision: the pond, the grassy area, the clocktower, and the raised concrete circular pad with the high half-wall, which apparently was a war memorial. Without being asked, I pointed to the spot in front of the wall and said, "Here."

Maximus took the map to his assistant and she quickly produced a printout of another map that was a blow-up of that concrete area. Maximus then laid that map out on the table and handed me a red pen. "I need to know precisely where each of us was standing, and also where Crofar is when he stops to speak."

I marked the map with circles for positions and labeled the circles with names. "I hope this works," I said. "When I had my vision, we were actually in these places. Don't you think what we are doing now is changing that future? I mean, how do we know *how* these holograms are going to change what happens in the future?"

"I thought about that too," Maximus agreed. "One thing's for sure, we *want* to change that future. Because, um, we all *die* and we don't want that."

"We could just skip the gassing event," Chase suggested. "That's my vote. I mean, let's ask ourselves, what insane maniac invites the town to a gassing?"

"You still don't get it, Bonehead," Hazel interjected. "We *are* skipping the gassing. If there is even going to be a gassing, we are making holograms of ourselves so we aren't there!"

"Who is the bonehead?" Chase asked, challenging Hazel, "I'll bet you a million dollars that John plans for us to be there, just not standing in those spots. Am I right, your kingship?" he finished, looking at me.

I put my head down and then looked at Maximus who took the hint and saved me from indirectly calling my girlfriend a bonehead. "My plan is to have a few of my people spread out to observe and relay events as they go down. Most of us, including you three, will be in this building behind the memorial." He pointed to the building in question on the map, which I never saw in my vision. He continued, "When we get the signal, that's when

267

we will need everyone engaged. Crofar's army won't be easy to bring down, even if we have a clear shot at Crofar himself."

"Sounds promising," Hazel said.

"Well, as long as we all end up alive I'll follow your plan," Chase said, giving in.

"So, do you guys want to start recording your holograms?" Maximus asked, diverting our attention to the contraption in the middle of the room.

"Yes," Hazel said, looking resigned to get this done and over with. "What should we record?"

I moved each of us into our places along the black wall and explained the whole scene as I remembered it. Then we rehearsed it a few times in real time until I thought we had it just right. Maximus's assistant played the part of Crofar and read his lines from a script that I had written out. When it all looked as I had seen it in the vision, I gave Maximus a nod and he moved back to the light table to determine the direction of the memorial and where the primary light source should be at that time of day. Then Maximus moved equipment around according to calculations made by his assistant, which took about ten minutes.

Once all the pieces were in place, there were ten more minutes of calculations and adjustments on the computer and finally, we were ready to start recording.

"Who wants to go first?" Maximus asked. Chase immediately volunteered. Maximus placed him in front of the black wall and made tiny corrections to his placement while looking at the computer screen. "Facial cues are important," Maximus warned Chase. "Luckily, all you need to do is look horrified for about five minutes and then you're done. I'll be standing where Crofar is so focus on me. I'll also be timing the action and I'll signal you twice, once when you get shot and drop and again when it's time for you to get up. Alright, silence on the set."

Chase relished his moment. He threw on a mask of a frightened teenager. He actually looked like he was scared senseless. Chase even added some body pivots into his acting to make it more lifelike. Maximus held up his timer a few times so Chase could see how much time was left. The minutes turned into seconds and the seconds counted down until there were twenty seconds left before the time he would be shot. We watched

269

anticipating the big signal letting Chase know it was time to fall over. When the signal came, Chase fell dramatically backwards onto the floor. Then he held his position of being dead until Maximus said, "Cut."

"Nice job!" I said, genuinely impressed with Chase's acting.

Chase stood up and bowed. "I'm glad I took all those drama classes," he said. "I thought they would just be time wasters but they were actually finally put to use."

Hazel quickly stepped into position for her five minute part, knowing that we were cutting all of this pretty close. But Maximus smiled at her and motioned us all to the computer where a special disk was being programmed with the digital 4D data. "Let's see how this one turned out before we make more," Maximus said. "If it's not real enough, there's no point in going any further with this idea."

Maximus placed the disk onto the floor in front of us. And then with a press of a button the hologram came to life. It looked exactly like Chase. It was like watching him do the recording all over again. I couldn't believe how real it looked so I walked up to it and examined every detail of the hologram. If I didn't know that this was a hologram, I would have had a conversation with holo-Chase. Chase gasped at how real the hologram looked and Hazel did too. Even Chase's fall was flawless. The T.F.G.'s technology had overcome the old problems of "floating" images that only look real from far away and in dim lighting. There was no doubt that, as long as the timing was right, the T.F.G. was going to fall for this.

High fives all the way around preceded Hazel's turn on stage. Another five minute performance worthy of an Oscar! I was riveted. Hazel moved her face in such a way when she was acting, that I moved my face as she moved hers. When she acted worried during the recording, I felt worried. It was as if we were parabatai and felt everything the other was feeling. Like he did with Chase, Maximus held up the timer with twenty seconds remaining and nodded his head when the time went out so that she could fake her death. Hazel fell down a bit too far to the side, making it harder for me to fit my fall between her body and Chase's. This would be another "tell" if after we fall, our holograms are overlapping.

271

"Well done! Very real, Hazel," Maximus said, complimenting her. I walked over to Hazel and lent her a hand. She grabbed it and stood up.

"Your turn, handsome. Let's see if you can top my acting skills," Hazel said to me as she took the gear off and helped put it on me. "Don't be terrible or you'll make me laugh," Hazel teased.

"Oh when this is over I'm going to show you who is boss of this town," I replied. She giggled and sat down at the table facing me.

"That one is done. Alright John, do you remember what to say and when to say it?" Maximus asked. "This is where the timing has to be perfect. No pressure."

"Yeah, none felt," I said with nerves tingling inside of me. Maximus gave me a hand signal and started the timer. I started by looking scared because Crofar was talking and reciting his speech as I remembered it from my vision. I felt kind of nervous performing in front of Chase and Hazel but I needed to focus on what to say and when to say it. I played back Crofar's words in my head and grimaced at Maximus like he was Crofar. If I remembered correctly from my vision, Crofar offers his deal and

272

then I speak and offer mine. I then let him laugh and talk back to me. Finally, I fell to the ground being careful to fall in a way that wouldn't overlap with holo-Chase or holo-Hazel.

Even though this was acting and wasn't real, it felt real. It felt as real as getting punched. I played it back in my mind and felt sure I had gotten the vision right. Soon enough we would all know for sure one way or the other.

"Alright, just one more," Maximus said, "mine. Give me a minute and then I'm going to need you, John, to take my position as Crofar and time me."

I walked over to Hazel to see what she thought of my acting. She gave me a hug and said, "That was really fantastic and I'm not joking."

"Thanks, Hazel," I said, "but you were better by a mile."

"Yo! John, nice work," Chase said loudly.

"Thanks bud," I returned, shaking his hand.

"Okay I'm ready," Maximus announced, "Stand exactly where I was standing, John. That way we are all looking at the same guy when this goes down."

"You hear that?" I whispered to Hazel, "He chose me to play Crofar and you know what that means? I'm his favorite."

"Yeah, right," she said, being a little flirty, "at least you're my favorite." I peeled myself away from her eyes and went to take Maximus's place.

"When I'm ready to act," he told me, "press the start button and the timer will automatically count down. Check on the timer periodically so that you can signal me at the right time to start faking my death."

Maximus went to his spot in front of the black wall and patted his clothes down to make them look less wrinkled. Then he fixed his brown hair, pressing it to the side of his head. When he was ready, he nodded. "Go," I said and started the timer. Maximus looked angry and defiant. His acting was spot on. As he continued his scene, I checked the timer, occasionally holding it up so he could see how much time he had left. Finally, I gave him the signal to drop and he did. A few seconds later, I called out, "Cut."

"How did I do?" Maximus wanted to know.

"You were stellar," I replied.

"Magnificent," Chase added.

"The performance of the decade," Hazel said, topping off our ridiculous string of compliments.

"You guys are full of it," he replied, "I like that." Then Maximus went over to his assistant and messed around with the disks that we were going to bring with us to the city center and, hopefully, use to defeat the T.F.G.

"Are you ready to finally beat the T.F.G.?" I asked Chase.

"I have no idea," Chase responded, "Our plan might fail and we could all get shot in the heads for real."

"You're right. I'm jinxing everyone," I replied, feeling the weight of responsibility for what we were about to do.

Chase shifted his weight to his other leg and tried again to make his point. "You're not jinxing us. You're just so sure about what is going to happen and it's not a guarantee."

"Well, knowing the future kind of lets me know what happens," I said.

Chase laughed at this. "Well, we've got to go set up the holograms soon before Crofar gets to where we need to be," he said. "I wonder if they have anything else to eat around here. I'm starving."

Maximus overheard Chase's plea for food, which is probably what Chase intended, and called out into the hallway for "gorp." In less than a minute, a giant bag of peanuts and raisins was making its way around the room.

"Not exactly what I had in mind," Chase muttered as he thrust his hand into the bag and pulled out a handful of the stuff and passed the bag to Hazel.

"Yum," she said, maybe seriously, maybe not. No one could tell.

"Holograms are ready," Maximus announced. "We can control them remotely with this device. I think we are almost ready to roll."

"Weapons?" Hazel asked.

"I'd prefer to let my guys do the heavy lifting in that department. I know you've proven yourself, Hazel, but none of you has the training for what I'm expecting today. Don't worry, I don't want anybody to be empty handed, but think defensive weaponry this time. Light and small." With that he yelled out some codeword into the hall and a minute later a soldier with a box was at the door. From this box Maximus distributed a black backpack to each of us. In each backpack was one small gun with ammo and one large sheathed knife. Only Hazel seemed disappointed as we adjusted our backpacks and put them on.

"This is the day," I said to everyone.

"Oh yeah it is," Chase responded.

CHAPTER 24

With minimal gear, the four of us piled into the Renegades' van and sat shoulder to shoulder with eight more of his crew, including the driver. Slowly, we crawled out of their base onto the quiet streets of Amber. On the way, I felt nervous. I didn't think it meant anything since I was nervous as a kid sitting in a waiting room to get a tooth pulled. There were things that comforted me. Hazel was of course one of them, and the other was our advantage. The T.F.G. had no idea what was about to happen today. They think that they are going to destroy us but actually it's them who are going to disintegrate, I thought.

It did not take long to get to the city center. Crofar wasn't there yet but we needed to hurry before he actually arrived. "I'll place the holograms," I told Maximus. He reached into his backpack and pulled out four discs, which would project the holograms when we were ready for them.

The van dropped Chase, Hazel, Maximus and me a block away from the park with the concrete memorial where we would put the discs. The rest of Maximus's elite crew sped off to be positioned elsewhere. We walked over the grassy lawn I remembered from my dream and then ascended the concrete steps where our fake selves would soon face off with our enemy. About four feet in front of the tall curved wall, I placed Maximus's hologram on the ground in front of me. I took a few steps to my right and then placed mine. Hazel was right next to me in the vision so I didn't need to move to place her hologram down. In last place was Chase who was between Maximus and me, two to three steps away from Hazel.

Once the holograms were placed in the correct order, we needed a way to hide them. Maximus pulled out four grey frisbee-looking things from his backpack and handed one to each of us. "These need to be placed carefully over the hologram discs so that the hole is centered. They should blend in with the concrete from Crofar's vantage point and still allow the holograms to project unimpeded."

"Brilliant!" Chase said, carefully centering his on top of the disc that would soon be him. Hazel and Maximus did the same, and I followed suit, positioning mine and then taking a look at the finished scene from where Crofar would be standing. Surprisingly, I could hardly see them, and that was even looking for them. Maximus is a genius, I thought.

We all got quiet for a moment, the reality sinking in that this is where we would die without these stand-ins. "Scared?" Hazel asked me, almost whispering.

"Scared? Why should I be scared? I can see the future, remember?" I reminded her, hoping that I sounded convincing.

"I can tell you're scared, John, and it's ok. Just because you're a guy doesn't mean you can't cry or be scared."

"Who said I was crying?" I asked defensively. Obviously my bravado was not convincing.

She rolled her eyes. "If you need help staying strong I'm here and so is Chase. Maybe even Maximus."

"Do I look like I need help staying strong?" I asked, mentally skidding downward.

Hazel must have known that her attempt to calm me was freaking me out, so she changed tactics. "Yeah, you look like you need to eat some steak and hit the gym," she joked.

"Look who's talking," I said, stuck in defense.

"Really? That's your comeback? You do realize I have more muscle than you," Hazel said, maybe joking, maybe not. It was kind of true.

Fortunately Maximus was there to bring us back to earth. He handed me one of his hack-proof walkie talkies and in a worried tone said, "I'm getting a signal from my army that there's a problem. I'm going to see if I can find out what's going on. You guys need to get into that building behind this wall. John, I will signal you on that device when it's time to move out. Until then, keep your heads down and stay alert! Anyone around here can be signaling back to the T.F.G."

That's when we noticed that there were people around, families mostly. Maybe they were coming to the park for a picnic. Maybe the adults were mind-controlled by the T.F.G. and they were coming to expose their kids to the gas. But if there wasn't going to be any gas and this was really a trap like Maximus said then the T.F.G. wouldn't be bringing the controlled to this place. Maybe Maximus was right and they were here to look out for us, just cleverly disguised to keep us from noticing. Suddenly the park felt very dangerous.

No one was close enough to identify us so we started walking toward the building while Maximus went back toward the area where the van dropped us. We all tried to blend in with the scene--just some friends hanging out at the park. The building looked like it was there to store maintenance equipment. It was all brick with a plain metal roof and a wide metal door that was locked. "How are we supposed to get in here?" Chase said looking around and jiggling the knob.

"Over here," Hazel said from around the corner of the building. Chase and I ran over just in time to see her smash a rock into a high window. "Give me a boost," she demanded, and I was immediately on all fours playing the part of a stepping stool. With her shoes planted on my back, she took her jacket off and used it to protect her hand as she pulled the glass away from the panes. When the glass was clear, she stuck her top half in for a look and then pushed herself off me and dove in. After a minute she threw out a two-step ladder that Chase and I promptly used to follow her inside. Once in, I leaned out and hoisted the ladder back up.

I looked around and saw one dim dusty room and a lot of junk. This was definitely a maintenance storage building. The small broken window was the only window. The door needed a key on the inside too so there was only one way for us to get out. "Great," Chase said sarcastically, seeing the same thing I was seeing.

Suddenly there was a sound at the door. Someone was trying to get in and this person had a key. The three of us stood there watching the doorknob, none of us breathing. As the door opened, we waited, all of us terrified that this would be a T.F.G. informant. The light streamed in as the door opened wider and the man caught sight of me, stopping in his tracks. He wore tan overalls and a large walkie talkie hung from the side of his belt. "Report, Willow Nine Nine. Is your location secure? Over." He put one hand on the walkie talkie and then started slowly backing out of the doorway like he was just going to leave. That's when I saw his other hand reach for a weapon tucked into his tool belt and before I could even blink, Hazel shot him in the head and he dropped like a rock.

Chase and I jumped from Hazel's sudden gunshot. "So much for laying low," Chase remarked calmly. He was getting used to being a target and having Hazel save us.

"I think Maximus also said, 'stay alert'," Hazel quipped as she ran over to check the guy that she just shot. He was definitely T.F.G. His walking talkie and firearm both had the T.F.G. insignia, and his costume coveralls were covering a soldier's uniform. Either they were looking for us, or they were getting into position and we beat them to this spot. Either way, the situation was teetering on disaster, since right before Hazel shot him he was being asked for a report about the security of his location.

"Either they heard the shot and they're going to come see what happened," I said, "or they didn't hear the shot and they're going to come see why this dude is not responding on his walkie talkie."

"So we're screwed, is what I'm hearing you say," Chase flipped back.

"Yep, that about sums it up," I concurred.

"I say we move locations," Hazel offered. At least someone was thinking.

"If they're moving their people into position too, we'll probably have the same problem wherever we go," Chase said, challenging Hazel. "Besides, there aren't too many hideouts around here from what I can see." Then he grabbed the dead soldier's walkie talkie and in his deepest stage voice called in, "Willow Nine Nine reporting...Secure....Over."

Frozen in shock at the brazenness of Chase's move, we stared at the walkie talkie and waited. "Copy, Willow Nine Nine. Stand by. Over."

"Unbelievable!" Hazel said with a huge smile on her face as Chase threw his fists into the air like he just scored the winning touchdown.

Before Chase could come down from his moment, the door burst open again. It was Maximus. Quickly and silently he closed the door behind him and put one finger to his lips. The brick building had muffled the gun shot so he had no idea what had just happened in there. "*What the....?*" he said out loud as soon as he saw the guy on the ground. Before anyone could

285

answer, he changed the subject. "Listen, we have a big problem," he said, "The T.F.G. have found my base and they attacked it this morning, shortly after we left. My army has taken a hit. A bunch of my people were taken off-guard and are now lost." Maximus paused to hold back his emotion. He took a deep breath and went on. "The rest are putting up a serious fight, but the upshot is that all we have here is the crew we rode down here with, and it's not going to get any better than that. No fortification like we had planned on."

"Maybe that's why we were able to just walk out of their base last night," I wondered out loud, "They followed us."

Maximus didn't say a word. He dropped his head with his hands on his hips. I could see a tear drop from his face as he turned away from us. A few seconds later, he faced us again. "It's going to be more difficult, that's for sure, but we still have a chance to take Crofar down here. The numbers are not going to be in our favor so we have to be smart."

"Dude, we have Hazel," Chase said trying to encourage himself and the rest of us. "And the holograms. We can do this."

"Hazel is going to need bigger guns," Hazel said, playing off Chase.

We all wanted to laugh but we didn't have it in us. Maximus looked at his watch and stared at it for a long time like he was thinking hard. That made me think about my dad's wristwatch and a rage began welling up inside me. I wanted to strangle Crofar with my bare hands and watch the life drain out of his eyes. And then I wanted to shoot him in every appendage and see how many bullets it would take to wipe that sick grin off his evil face. And then I wanted to punch his lifeless body until I was too tired to punch it anymore.

Maximus stopped my descent into hell when he started thinking out loud. "I've got one set of eyes on the platform where the holograms are. I've got a driver. I've got two lookouts on each of the three streets that feeds this place. I can bring in three guys so we have only one lookout on each street. The problem is that I wanted to take Crofar out on the street, before he even makes it here. No sense in hoping he would be fooled by the holograms, you know? Now we have to hope he will be fooled by the holograms because I just don't have the manpower, especially since we know he's flanked by his own army almost everywhere he goes."

"If Crofar's army is at your base right now, he's going to know we have a skeleton crew here," I said. "I guess that's why in my vision he is standing there facing us alone. I mean, his guys were pretty far behind him, in the grassy area."

"That's our only real shot at this point, I think," Maximus agreed, "a sniper attack on Crofar as he's talking to the holograms. If we try to engage his army, or worse, if his army engages us before the meeting on the memorial, we are toast."

"What I don't get," Chase said, "is why we are standing on that platform in the first place."

"That's easy when you think about it," I said. "We lure Crofar to the top of the memorial so that the Renegades can get a crack at him, but he knows that's what we are going to try to do so he attacks the Renegade base so we have no army to save us. Then he marches up here and shoots us."

"But how does he *know* all of this?" Chase asked, pressing his point.

"Holy crap, Chase, you might be onto something," I said. "Is it possible that Crofar has the same ability I have? I mean, do you think that he has dream-visions of the future too? That would explain a lot!"

Maximus squinted his eyes and turned his head to the left, staring off into space. I came to recognize that as his thinking pose. "So, Crofar knew you would make it into his base so he planted a fake newspaper article about the gas."

"And he knew he would be meeting the four of us on that concrete memorial, which is why he is making sure we have no backup," I added.

"But he isn't expecting holograms, is he?" Chase asked. "I mean, did he dream about meeting *us*, or did he dream about meeting *holo*-us?"

"I have no idea!" I admitted. "This future-seeing thing is boggling!"

"Wait," Hazel broke in, "Dreamers dream from their own point of view, right? John, in your dream, you were really there, right?" She didn't wait for a reply. "So, we made the holograms and that's a change, but Crofar would have dreamed what you dreamed, unless he's sleeping right now just for the intel."

"He's not sleeping now," Maximus said, "I can tell you that. My lookout on First Street just notified me that he's on his way here."

"So, do we have a plan?" Chase asked, "I'm still hoping not to be shot in the head today."

"This dude," Hazel said pointing to the dead guy on the floor, "is supposed to have secured this location, and we are pretty sure that the T.F.G. thinks he has succeeded. That means we are safe in here, for a little while, I hope."

"Okay, so I move my guys--I've got six that are mobile--into places with a clean shot of Crofar on the platform," Maximus said. "You three stay in here until you get my signal. But be ready to fight. I'm not sure what his army will do when Crofar goes down."

"We'll be ready," Hazel said.

"Yep," Chase agreed, "at least we have a chance."

While Maximus was talking, I noticed a tiny bit of sunlight coming through the roof. Sunbeams were floating in the narrow strip of light that landed on a bright red gas tank, and I watched them dance as an idea came together in my mind. As soon as Maximus was out of there, I would tell my friends. "Let's get this in motion," I told Maximus. "And if it doesn't turn out well, thanks for everything. We wouldn't have made it this far without you."

"Don't count us out, yet," Maximus said in response. "We might be outnumbered, but my finest crew is here, and that includes you three. It's been an honor to work with you, and I'm planning on working with you still when this little laughing monster is no more." With that, Maximus slipped out the door and I barely let it close before I started to tell my friends my plan.

"I have an idea," I started. "We can help Max and his guys if we create a diversion. You know, pull some of Crofar's army off Crofar so maybe we have a better shot."

"How are we going to do that?" Chase asked.

"I think I know what you're thinking," Hazel said, following my eyes to the gas tank in the middle of the room.

"Help me with this ladder," I said, moving piles of junk that had buried a tall fold-up ladder laying sideways under the broken window. Chase and Hazel both jumped in and started moving stuff out of the way so we could get the ladder out.

"What are we going to do with this?" Chase asked, freeing the ladder from its dusty post and helping me stretch it out in a clear spot.

"I want to get up to that hole in the roof and see if we can use it to see what's going on out there," I said.

"That's a pretty small hole," Chase said, grabbing the ladder and positioning it under the hole. The next thing I knew, he was up the ladder with a crowbar. He shoved the crowbar into the hole and peeled back the metal roof in every direction. Suddenly we had a fantastic view over the high wall to the spot where Crofar would soon be standing. "There," Chase said, satisfied with his contribution, "Now what?"

I climbed the ladder and surveyed all that I could see. It was starting to get windy. The families we saw earlier were nowhere to be seen. To our right was a cluster of shrubs, to our left was a statue of a soldier on a horse. There were trees dotting the landscape. I checked the time on the clocktower straight away and it showed me that we had ten minutes before Crofar would be climbing up the steps onto the concrete platform. This was an awesome view of the action that would soon be taking place. The only thing we couldn't see was the row of holograms that Crofar would try to kill. I wished I could see his face when he realizes that he is a pathetic fool, shooting bullets at the air.

I climbed down and went over to the gas can, lifting it up. It was about half full. I looked around to see what else we could use to distract the T.F.G. and help Maximus's snipers fulfil their mission and make it out of here alive. I wanted rags and empty bottles. And a catapult, which seemed kind of unlikely to be laying around a maintenance shed.

"I sure am thirsty," I said, turning to my friends, "does anyone have a Molotov cocktail?"

Chase's eyes got huge and he immediately started rummaging through the junk in the shed to find bottles. Hazel got it too and almost instantly produced a pile of dirty rags and paper towels from a trash can in the corner. In two minutes, we were pouring gas and motor oil into empty coke bottles and stuffing rags and paper towels into their narrow necks. We had enough material to make nine bombs.

293

"Okay," I said, "I'm thinking we give Crofar a couple minutes of his ridiculous speech and if Maximus hasn't killed him by then, we hurl these from the roof into those shrubs on the right. Whose got the best arm?"

"Obviously, you are talking about me," Chase answered, as he started to go up the ladder again.

"Wait!" Hazel insisted, pulling Chase down and moving him out of the way. "At least let me get up there for a second and see the lay of the land."

"Well, hurry up," he replied, "we don't have all day."

"No we don't," Hazel said from the lookout atop the ladder, "I think I see Crofar and his army approaching. Yep, they are walking this way. I'd say about twenty soldiers."

"Get out of the way, Hazel," Chase said impatiently, "Let me get up there!"

"Hold on, Chase," I ordered. "Hazel, do you see the statue on the left? On my signal, I want you to sprint to that statue and take cover. I want you to take out Crofar as soon as you have a clean shot of him. He's the priority target. I'll cover you from behind, and Chase will cover you from above. And Chase, don't start hurling bombs until I tell you, got it? Okay, let's get into position."

Hazel came down the ladder and all three of us carefully put the bombs in an empty bucket. Hazel went to the door, Chase went up the ladder and I stood below him with the bucket of bombs and a lighter. "Does everyone have their weapons loaded?" I asked.

"Check," they each said in unison.

"We've only got about a minute," I alerted them after checking my watch, "Does everyone know what to do?"

"Crofar is about to go up the steps," Chase said from the lookout. "I sure hope Maximus has the holograms coming on. I guess we'll find out. He's going up." After a brief moment of silence, Chase said, "It must be working--he's talking and laughing! His army is spread out behind him. They're not expecting anything, the way they are casually holding their guns."

"Let's surprise them, then," I said impatiently, lighting one of the bombs and handing it to Chase. He took it from my hand and threw it hard through the hole in the roof. I could hear the glass break. His precision must have been a surprise even to him, because in the most stunned expression I had ever seen on him, he reported that the bushes were on fire and that ten soldiers were running toward them to see what was going on. "Go!" I told Hazel, and she was out the door as a burst of gunfire erupted outside. "What's going on?" I yelled to Chase, thinking the worst.

"They are randomly shooting at the hedge where the fire is, John. It's working!"

"Can you see Hazel?" I asked. "Is she at the statue? Is she safe?"

"She's at the statue. No one knows she is there."

"This sucks that I can't see what's going on," I said. "I'm going out there to back up Hazel. I need you to cover me. But especially her."

"I won't let you down, my friend," Chase said in reply. "Hurry the hell up!"

As soon as I left the maintenance shed I could hear trouble. Two of the soldiers that had split off from the group were talking to each other and approaching the shed. I turned the corner before they could see me, but I had no way of warning Chase. They would definitely see the broken window and get

296

suspicious. It was only a matter of time before Chase would be discovered. I reached into my pocket and felt the device that Maximus had given me to signal him for help. Before I could even get it out of my pocket, I heard a single gunshot coming from Hazel's position and then all hell broke loose.

One after the other, flaming bottles came flying out of the roof of the shed. Gunshots rang out in every direction. Hazel was running back to the door of the shed from the statue and almost ran me over. We collided and landed on the ground together. "Are you okay?" I asked, grasping her hands and pulling us both up off the ground. "Did you hit Crofar?" I practically had to shout over all the gunfire as we pressed ourselves against the wall.

"No, that wasn't me," Hazel said, breathing hard. "Maximus took a shot at Crofar from the trees just past the statue where I was. We saw each other first and he motioned for me to wait. I shouldn't have listened. I think he's been shot. Maximus, I mean. I think Maximus has been shot. I was taking fire too but Chase started throwing those bombs and that gave me just enough time to break free and bump into you. Literally." Then she casually lifted her gun and shot a soldier that was coming up behind me. "C'mon, let's get back into the shed."

"Hopefully Chase won't shoot us," I said as we peered around the corner making sure the coast was clear. One glance and zero hesitation and Hazel was sprinting to the door with me hot on her heels. We burst inside to find Chase on top of the ladder taking shots at T.F.G. soldiers through the hole in the roof. When he heard us, he reeled around with his gun so fast that the ladder went sideways throwing Chase to the floor and into a pile of junk.

"Welcome home, roomies," he groaned. "Want some dinner?"

Hazel ran over to him, running her hands along his arms and legs, looking for breaks. "That must have hurt," she said, helping him up and brushing off his clothes while he groaned some more.

"Hazel thinks Maximus was shot," I said, ignoring Chase's pain. "Did you see anything?"

Chase squeezed his eyes together and tears fell. "I saw everything," he said. "He wasn't just shot. He was pummeled with bullets. As soon as he fired at Crofar, they just filled him with bullets. He must have known that was going to happen."

Hazel looked at me and tears filled her eyes too. "He did it to save me. We were so focused on drawing attention away from Crofar that we made his job harder! He saw me out there and was probably trying to keep Crofar's army from seeing me too."

I felt gut punched. This had been my idea and now maybe I was responsible for Maximus being dead. It was more than I could bear and I dropped to the ground with my head in my hands. I was so distraught that I didn't even notice an escalation in gunfire. But Hazel had. She straightened out the ladder and climbed to the top, peering through the peeled away metal.

"I don't believe it," she said, "the Renegades are here!"

CHAPTER 25

Chase perked up and loaded his weapon, reaching up to hand it off to Hazel. Then he ran over to the dead soldier on the floor and picked up his weapon too, checking his body for more ammunition. He was so steady and determined--it was like Chase wasn't even Chase. My two best friends were not going to be defeated by these T.F.G. monsters. They still had hope.

All I had was bitter anger. *Maximus is shot. He's dead. This can't be happening!* I couldn't move a muscle. Someone might as well have put me in a wheelchair. I was stunned into paralysis. I felt like someone was continuously punching me in the gut. All sounds were drowned out as I sat there on the floor of that shed, tears dripped onto my shirt and the floor as my body rocked back and forth. Crofar was going to pay for this. I had to make sure that Crofar paid. Suddenly, almost like I was under the control of someone else, I picked up my knife and gripped it so hard that my nerves started to burn. I was so mad and fired up that I sprinted out the door with all my strength, determined to kill Crofar.

"John, *NO!*" I heard Chase yell as if he could stop me. I sprinted to the statue where Hazel had gone earlier, hoping she would cover me from the hole in the roof. From there I could see a battlefield where there was once a park. Bodies were strewn on the grassy lawn. Bullets were flying over them. The Renegades were taking cover behind trees on the west side of the park and the T.F.G. soldiers that were still standing were spread out on the east side, hiding behind stubby concrete pylons spaced out along the edge to keep cars out. A couple of trees and shrubs were still burning after Chase's bomb-throwing helped Hazel make it back safely to the shed. I thought I would have to thank him for that if we made it out of there alive.

All I wanted at that moment was to get my hands on Crofar, but first I had to find him. That's when I noticed a cluster of T.F.G. soldiers just behind the wall on the far side of the concrete platform. None of them were firing and they were just out of Hazel's site so she couldn't get to them from her roof shelter. They must have been protecting Crofar, I thought. Maybe he was injured. Maybe I would finish him off. Then I would be satisfied.

To my right the concrete platform was empty. The only things on it were the hollow grey frisbees that covered the discs where our holo-selves once stood. I could see that the curved wall would shield me and I could get really close to their location, but I wasn't going to be able to take them all with my knife. I needed help. I knew that Hazel could see the statue from her location so I climbed up as high as I could get onto the platform under the horse. I craned my neck to see the hole that Chase had made in the metal roof and with a little effort to maneuver myself around the legs of the bronze horse, I could see Hazel. My heart skipped a beat. She was looking at me too.

I motioned to her in the direction of Crofar and his guards. She nodded that she understood and her head disappeared. I waited to see what she would do, and I didn't have to wait long. A flaming bottle came shooting out of the hole and landed right in the middle of the cluster of guards and they scattered. As they scurried across the lawn like rats I could see them drop. The Renegades were excellent sharpshooters. One by

302

one, the whole unit was whittled down to the two that stayed put--Crofar and his faithful bodyguard. The odds were not in my favor but I started to charge them anyway.

I almost made it when the bodyguard fired a shot at me. But he missed. The bullet he fired hit the wall and ricocheted into Crofar's arm. The bullet lodged into Crofar's dominant arm, which was holding a gun. Crofar backed up as his gun fell to the ground. The bodyguard stared at Crofar in confusion and then disbelief as it dawned on him that *he* had shot Crofar. I seized the moment and picked up Crofar's gun, swinging my arms around and pointing the gun at the bodyguard. "*Drop it!*" I screamed at the top of my lungs.

"It's you or me, kid," he replied, raising his gun. But with his arm about half way up, like it was happening in slow motion, I watched his face turn from confidence to disbelief to resignation. He dropped his gun and drew his hands to his gut where blood was pouring out, and then he slumped to the ground. Behind him was Hazel, her gun extended at the end of her outstretched arms. She had saved me again.

We shared a quick glance and then we both swung our guns around to Crofar. He threw his arms in front of him in one of those automatic gestures, like he was going to block bullets with his hands. He wasn't laughing when he pleaded for his life. "I'll offer you a deal if you spare my life," he blurted out, looking between me and Hazel, no doubt peeing his pants.

"I'm tired of your deals," I screamed, "and I can hardly imagine you having anything we want *more* than killing you! So how about you to do as I say instead, huh? You tell your little soldiers to stop firing or I'll shoot you right now."

He squinted his evil eyes and at least pretended to capitulate. "Alright, you win. I need to use my walkie talkie to give my army the signal to stand down. It's a coded message," he said. I nodded for him to send the signal as I raised my gun to his head in case he tried something. He slowly lowered one hand to his radio, brought it up to his mouth, and moved his index finger to push the button.

"I'm warning you, you tricky bastard," I said, watching him closely and putting my finger on the trigger. "If you want to live you will stop this war now." Hazel tensed up too and was ready to fire.

"Stop firing," Crofar called into the device, "Code ZA5W." Just like that, the gunshots from the T.F.G. soldiers stopped, but the Renegades were still firing. I reached into my pocket and withdrew the device that Maximus had given to me. I wasn't sure it would get to anyone, but I tried it anyway.

"This is John Williams," I called into the device. "I have Crofar in custody. Stand down. Over." Immediately, all gunfire stopped. I suddenly felt like I was about ten feet tall. "Now," I said to Crofar, "I want all T.F.G. weapons in a pile right by that trash container over there. See it? Have your men come out one by one, throw their weapons down there and move to the middle of the lawn with their hands up. I'm not kidding. I want every weapon they have. Guns. Knives. Grenades. Everything."

Crofar hesitated and looked over toward the pylons where his army was hunkered down, and then to the trees where the Renegades were hiding. "How am I supposed to trust the Renegades?" he asked. "They're just a bunch of good-for-nothing thugs. They're the whole problem with this world! They go

305

around acting like stupid people should have rights! Well, stupid people do stupid things! They think this or that is going to make them happy, but that just messes with the natural order. If you don't know the natural order, you're bound to mess with it! That's why I invented the T.F.G. in the first place. I can make people happy! I can give people what they really want, what they really need, ORDER!"

Crofar was acting like a maniac again, smiling and laughing and gesticulating wildly. Hazel was ready to shoot him at any second. I looked over to her and tried to discourage her with my eyes. I didn't want Crofar to know that I wanted him alive, but I was pretty sure Hazel knew what I was thinking.

"You're making a huge mistake," he ranted on, "There's still time for you to join me! Once we develop and administer the gas, we won't need guns or an army because everyone, absolutely everyone, will be happy! We are so close!"

I fell into the trap of trying to reason with a madman. "What about people like me? And my parents? You told me we were immune. Well, if we are immune, others are too. Besides, who are you to say what the natural order is? Who are you to

306

decide what should make everyone happy? Who are you to decide even that everyone should be happy? Maybe there are things that matter beyond happiness! Like the truth! Like real friends who would do anything for you! Like love!" I was screaming by the time I was finished.

Hazel's eyes were wide and fixed on me now, instead of Crofar. She looked surprised. I had never told her about my meeting with Crofar and what he told me about my immunity. I had never tried to talk to her about how I felt about the T.F.G., besides the fact that they had killed my parents. Hell, I didn't even know how I felt about their peace-inducing mind-control myself, until I heard these words come out of my mouth right then and there.

"Well said, Socrates!" I heard Chase say as he approached from behind me, gun drawn and pointed at Crofar. "Now do what the man, said, Crofar the Clown. Weapons in a pile by the trash can. Now!"

Suddenly a bullet grazed Chase's arm and he flattened himself to the ground, looking around for its source. Hazel immediately turned and shot the bodyguard, this time in the head, who had managed to pull out a small handgun and fire it. I clenched my teeth in rage and shot Crofar in the leg. "I'm not bluffing. If your people fire another bullet at my team, I'll shoot you in the head. I don't know about you, but that would make *me* happy!"

Crofar grimaced from the pain and picked up his radio, breathing hard as he gave the instructions. With Hazel's gun trained on Crofar, Chase and I watched his people come out one by one, dropping their weapons and assembling in the grassy clearing. When the last T.F.G. soldier emerged from the pylons, the Renegades swept their dugout and surrounded their prisoners.

"All clear," came from nowhere, until I realized it was coming from the device that Maximus gave me.

"Excellent," I replied into the device. "Time to un-brainwash this world." Turning then to Crofar, I said, "You. You are going with us to your base. And this time, you will help us undo the mess that you have made."

"I'll tell you how to set all those puny minds free if that's what you want," he replied. "But I'll rise again, John, and I will be avenged. Maybe when you're all grown up, you will even see that I was right."

I couldn't believe what he was saying. Why would anyone want someone else to control them? And what was he going to avenge? People taking back control over their own lives? With Hazel and Chase still pointing guns at him, I pulled Crofar up onto his feet and he hobbled onto his good leg, cringing as he limped a few feet ahead. "Let's see how you like being controlled, shall we. Maybe you'll see that you were wrong!"

With the help of a sturdy branch that Chase pulled out of the bushes, Crofar limped alongside me and my friends as we headed towards the base. The Renegades followed behind, herding their T.F.G. prisoners whose hands they had bound together at their backs. The streets were empty and the only sound as we walked was the howling afternoon wind. In less than half an hour, we had reached the entrance to the base, which was still without a door. We simply walked in.

Crofar led us down familiar corridors to a lab filled with many computers. He started talking about the lab as if we were on a tour. "That liquid brewing on the middle counter is of course my favorite brainwashing mechanism. The computers around it are used to control the people we have treated with the serum. Feel free to set your little dumb teenage minds to bringing havoc back to the world."

"Why don't you just tell us, oh brilliant one," Hazel said. "Last time I checked, the dumb teenagers were holding a gun to your sorry head."

Crofar started to laugh. "There's only one way to un-do all of my good work. And I can't help you with that. You need access to the mainframe and in order to get that you have to draw an emblem which is the password. Once you draw the correct emblem on the touch screen and get in, it's just a matter of deleting each file, one for every person that has taken the serum."

"That doesn't sound so hard," Chase said, "What's the password?"

"I told you," he replied, snickering, "it's an emblem. You have to draw it."

"Fine! What's the emblem?" I yelled, slamming a piece of paper and pencil in front of Crofar. "Draw it for us!"

Crofar stopped laughing. "I don't know it," he said sinisterly. "There is only one person in the world who knows the password and that person is not me."

"Well who the hell is it?" I demanded to know. "Why should we not shoot you right now, since you don't know the password that we need. Or maybe you know who can help us, so you can stay alive another minute!" I was furious. Somehow this guy thinks he can still win as he stares down the barrel of a gun.

I grabbed the screen and started to draw a random emblem. I would try shapes all day until I landed on the right one. I started off by drawing some square shapes and zigzags. They didn't unlock the system, which automatically cleared the sketch pad prompting me to try again. I was about to draw every shape that I could think of from a circle to a triquetra when Chase stopped me. "I wouldn't do that, John. Most systems lock you out if you try a password unsuccessfully more than a few times."

I turned to Crofar again, "If you don't tell us what the shape is, Chase will be happy to shoot you in your other leg."

"Will that help you free any minds?" he replied, taunting me. "Besides, John, surely you know you are likely to catch more

flies with honey than vinegar. Why don't you offer me something
I want, rather than threaten me with something I don't want."

"I wouldn't give you a dime, even if I had a million
dollars!" I shouted, sinking into a desperate frustration. I sat down
on the swivel chair in front of the computer with my head in my
hands. *Money, is that what this is about? Controlling people's minds for
money?* Or maybe this was a hint. Crofar was a diabolical vile man.
I could imagine him toying with us by giving hints. So maybe the
emblem was a dollar sign. But what if I was wrong? Some dollar
signs have two lines, some have one. But that's just too easy, I
thought, especially since Crofar seemed so confident that we
wouldn't figure it out. Besides, how could I test out any shape
without risking getting locked out?

The more I tried to think about shapes, the more my
mind meandered back to how things were before, with my mom
and dad getting ice cream, and afternoons doing homework at
Chase's, walking home through the scary alley that I didn't know
was the Renegades' base, and the drives through Amber City
before I had ever even heard of the Tracker for Globe. But no
matter what happened here, I knew things would never be the

same again. Even if we defeated these idiotic snakes and destroyed all the serum and deleted all the files of programming, somehow I would have to go on without my parents, and without a purpose. At least my mom had left me something--the wallet--with pictures and money and the letter on the jump drive. I would get by.

The wallet! Suddenly I remembered that the wallet my mom had given me was embellished with that strange circular symbol. I remember tracing it out with my finger, wondering what it might mean. She told me that she had hacked into the T.F.G. database, and now it seemed possible that she knew this symbol was somehow the key to dismantling their mind-controlling enterprise, even if she didn't know how. I started to think that there was more to her passing this wallet onto me than the pictures and the money.

I shot out of my chair, sending it rolling backward into the wall. "I'll be right back. Everybody wait here! If he moves, kill him," I said to Hazel, winking slyly so she knew that I was only trying to scare Crofar. I ran through the base knocking over every bottle of serum that I could on the way.

313

When I got to the edge of the woods just before our little rental house, I stopped. Crofar knew we would be at the park today and he had every reason to think he would kill us there. So I was pretty sure I wouldn't run into any of his guards at the house. Still, I wanted to make sure. It looked fine from the outside. No one was guarding the door so I cautiously let myself in. I quickly walked toward my room but a guy was standing in the hallway. "Who are you?" I asked, looking him over for a gun.

"I'm your neighbor," the man said, smiling in that mindless way. I could see he was just a victim of Crofar's generic happiness. "I heard a noise and wanted to make sure everything was okay over here. You kids have been gone awhile."

"Thank you," I said, "That's very thoughtful of you. We are fine, though. I just ran home to pick something up. Then I'll be off again." I smiled broadly as I spoke, hoping he would think I was under control too.

"Okay," he replied, "Glad to know you're all okay. You're all okay, right?"

"Right!" I said cheerfully. "Let's talk again tomorrow. I've got to be on my way."

He seemed to take the hint and headed to the door. I watched him hoping he would just leave, but of course he did not. He turned around with a small handgun and told me that I was not supposed to be here and that he had better stop me from doing any more harm. His hand was shaking but he was going to do what he was supposed to do.

"You don't want to do that," I told him, remembering how my dad was able to control the doctor that was trying to give me the serum. "You will not shoot me," I added. His gun hand was shaking violently at that point and beads of sweat were falling from his head. I kept up the pressure. "You never wanted to hurt anyone. That's just not you."

Tears began streaming from his eyes and his gun fell to the ground. It worked! He collapsed in a heap and sobbed uncontrollably. I snatched the gun while I had the chance and left him there to retrieve the wallet. I grabbed the wallet from my dresser and ran past him back out the door. I felt sorry for this man, but also hopeful. Maybe people's minds were stronger than Crofar thought. Maybe a person's 'nature' could still find a way through.

With my wallet in hand, I ran back to the T.F.G. base. I couldn't wait to see if the insignia worked. It would be a miracle if it was the key to unlocking a new world. "I think I have it," I declared, skidding into the lab. I displayed the wallet for Hazel and Chase as if it were a handful of diamonds. Crofar tried to see what I was so excited about but Hazel forced him back to his chair. His bleeding had stopped but he looked weak. I went to the sketch pad and placed the wallet directly on it so that the pattern was facedown on the screen. As soon as the circular pattern registered with the computer, a message popped up on the screen. It read, "Welcome Crofar. Are you sure you want to permanently delete all files?"

"No friggin way," Chase said excitedly. I clicked on the 'yes' button and the computer screen displayed file icons flying into the trash bin in the bottom right-hand corner. Every file that entered the trash can released another person from the bondage and emptiness of Crofar's "happiness." The entire world was being unlocked. We were all free and out of the grasp of Crofar. There was cheering and excitement behind me so I joined in. We were jumping up and down, high-fiving each other, and shouting

316

with glee. "Oh my god, it's over," Hazel cried in excitement. She then pulled me in for a kiss as if it were New Year's Eve and the clock just struck midnight.

We were all so mesmerized by the computer screen and reveling in our accomplishment that we had completely forgotten about Crofar. I looked down to the chair where he was sitting and the only thing on it was a bloodstain from his wounded leg. I looked around the room and saw only Renegades, smiling and laughing. Some were even dancing. "Quiet!" I yelled. "Crofar is gone!" Before anyone else could say a word or leave the lab to look for him, the whole damn base powered down. No light, no sound. No animated files flying into the virtual trash.

We all stood there in complete darkness for a minute, immobile. I could feel my own heart beating. I could hear Hazel breathing next to me. I could smell that electronics smell from all the computers and the weird odor of all that spilt serum. Finally, a voice. It was Chase's. "Not good," he said.

Acknowledgements

I would like to thank the following people for their immeasurable assistance in helping to make this dream a reality.

Mom, thank you for supporting my passion unconditionally and for encouraging me to write another word when I wanted to quit. Your endless discussions helping me decide the path of the story were so helpful. Thank you for everything. I love you so much.

My dad, sisters, Sarah and Gabby, plus all my friends- thank you for listening to me talk about this book for the past four years! And for those of you that competed in the social media contest to name Hazel, thank you! It was fun watching her be named.

Gina Calderone, thank you for your suggestions and rewrites on this novel. You are an unbelievable editor and without your help, the main character would have been in big trouble.

Bubbie Jeanie Bernstein thank you for your amazing enthusiasm and for editing each chapter of my book. Your positive comments after made me feel great about how I could make my readers feel.

Aunt Joanna & Uncle Mike, thank you for a very generous birthday gift which helped cover some of my costs. Also, thank you, Aunt Joanna, for editing some of my earlier chapters.

Steve Harris with CSG Literary Partners/MDM Management, thank you for reviewing my earlier documents when I was pitching this book to agents and publishers.

Jason Simon, thank you for the awesome cover image and really listening and understanding how I wanted my novel to look.

I hope you enjoy reading about John, Chase, and Hazel as much as I enjoyed writing about them!

About the Author

Zachary was born and is being raised in Scottsdale, AZ. At the age of fourteen, he recently completed his first novel, "The Uncontrolled." This is the young author's second venture into the world of publishing. In 2017, he wrote, directed, and starred in a video about the Fourth Amendment, winning first place in the Scottsdale Mayor's Constitutional Contest. He has also appeared at Carnegie Hall for the New York Pops 2016 Gala and has received two National Youth Award nominations for his role in community theater productions. He is the drummer of a teenage band and plays club soccer. His hope is to become a better writer and influence others to read.

To learn more about Zachary and his book, please visit:
Website: theuncontrolled.wixsite.com
Email: zachary.astrowsky@yahoo.com
Follow: the_uncontrolled_novel on Instagram

CPSIA information can be obtained
at www.ICGtesting.com
Printed in the USA
LVHW111801301018
595356LV00006B/536/P